To
SiD

Head to Head

Enjoy Reading

Head To Head

From

Suzanne Gill

x

Head to Head

Suzanne Gill

Published by www.lulu.com

© Copyright Suzanne Gill 2016

HEAD TO HEAD

All rights reserved.

The right of Suzanne Gill to be identified as the author of this work has been asserted in accordance with the Copyright, Designs, and Patents Act 1988.

No part of this publication may be reproduced, stored in a retrieval system, or transmitted, in any form or by any means, electronic, mechanical, photocopying, recording, or otherwise, nor translated into a machine language, without the written permission of the publisher.

This is a work of fiction. Names and characters are a product of the author's imaginations and any resemblance to actual persons, living or dead, events and organisations is purely coincidental.

Condition of sale

This book is sold subject to the condition that it shall not, by way of trade or otherwise, be lent, re-sold, hired out or otherwise circulated in any form of binding or cover other than that in which it is published and without a similar condition including this condition being imposed on the subsequent purchaser.

ISBN 978-1-326-81503-5

Book formatted by www. bookformatting. co. uk.

Contents

24th September Reflection 1

The Woods 10

Hunger 20

The Mist 25

Abandonment 29

Intruder 42

False Calm 46

Trepidation 52

Confrontation 57

A Miraculous Vision 65

Confirmation 70

Ouija 81

Sudden Popularity 90

November 2 Jessica's Warning 97

Father McDade 109

Family Support 115

Joseph 122

Possession 128

The Motley Trio 137

Loathing 148

The Light 154

Acknowledgements

Eileen Gill. Thanks for becoming a light shining through the darkest times of my life.

Your strength and love helped me carry on through my ordeal.

When my world was falling apart you were the only one who stood by me.

For this I am eternally grateful to have a wonderful aunt as amazing as you.

love you x

Thank you to Sandra Brannigan & Francesca Hadwin for all your hard work and effort to help me write Head to Head.

I couldn't have done it without you both x

24th September
Reflection

Little Jessica was squirming within the burlap sack as it swung back and forth in the wind. Her cries emanated from within the rough fabric. She had been hastily tied up to a twisted branch. I could just touch the bottom of the sack as it swung past my head. I tried to time my jumps with the blowy gusts, to grab it at the lowest part of its sway. Each time the gales defeated me, pulling her just out of reach.

Over the squall I shouted to her, telling her I would help her and that everything would be okay. She pleaded for help repeatedly, my helplessness was growing beyond tolerable limits. The rope squeaked and groaned over the rough bark, its eerie sound making a mockery of my attempts. I would need to take a run at it. Taking several steps back through the undergrowth, I prepared myself. When the twisting sack neared its highest point, I broke into a run. Jumping just as it came down from its horrid sway, I reached for it and grabbed a bit of fabric in both hands.

An almighty crack followed as the branch snapped and gave way. The sack containing Jessica fell on me and we both landed in a heap onto some twigs which were laying on the uneven ground. Jessica was now beside herself and screaming. I tried to reassure her it was me, but she wouldn't be settled. Now I feared she'd been injured by the branch as it fell. Aching from the fall didn't stop me from scrambling for the knots at the top of sack. My hands were shaking as I fumbled with the ties, made worse by Jessica's kicking and writhing in panic.

Finally, having loosened the cords, I stretched the fabric open at the top and reached through to pull her out of her small, burlap prison. Pulling her out, I screamed in horror. It wasn't Jessica. It was the skeletal remains of a woman, her straggly hair whipped about in the wind. As I feared it couldn't get any worse, the skull turned towards me. It cackled with delight. Repulsed, I threw it back down to the ground and jumped away from it. I broke into a run towards the dim light at the back of the pub. I'd only covered a short distance when I was stopped in my tracks.

'You think you're so fucking clever!' it screeched before resuming its acrid laughter.

Jarred awake, I sat straight up in my bed. I was soaked through to the skin with sweat, the sheets sticking to my skin. Tears were streaming down my face and my eyes burnt from weeping. My panic was full on, the dream so real, the cackle still resonating in my mind. I tried to slow my heartbeat, but it continued to drum in my ears. The nightmares were worsening as each night passed.

Once again sleep had failed me, a good night's rest had been replaced by another dreadful dream. Every time I tried to relax, a magnitude of haunting visions came rushing to my mind. Of Joseph, standing in the darkness waiting for me and of children and women screaming. I couldn't shut off. Over the past nine days at the Wheatsheaf Hotel, Joseph had made me more than aware of his evil presence and malicious doings. I felt a blurring of reality. Somewhere within the short span of just over a week, my world had completely turned upside down. Even with family around me, I still felt alone and often wondered if people would remain physically standing near to me if they knew what I had seen and dealt with. More than likely, they would scurry a safe distance away.

So here I was, on a different plane to the rest of the population on the planet, craving a mundane existence. I longed for the normality of any individual going about their daily business. I couldn't bear to be alone and felt so uncertain about everything. I didn't know what to do, this nightmare had taken a lot out of me. I didn't feel safe anymore… anywhere. My body seemed to be moving in slow motion, but my mind was alive with thoughts. Every time I tried to make sense of what had happened, my mind began to run over and over the events as if they were running in a loop. From meeting Simon and Shirley, the psychics called in for a second opinion, to the death threats Simon had warned me about, I realized the visions and the feelings he had picked up on, mirrored what I had seen and felt. It was hard to come to terms with all that had taken place and I felt as if I had been shell shocked.

Looking back to the days before meeting all the entities at the Wheatsheaf, I realized I'd previously lived in a sheltered bubble. Dealing with the spirit world all my life, good, bad and otherwise, I felt nothing would surprise me. But normally, with most of spirits, I had an inkling of their presence. Sometimes they came in dreams, in a waking state they came as rapid snapshots. Not Joseph though, oh no... nothing... no forewarning, no dreams or premonitions, just full on evil in the blink of an eye. With one ghastly stare he had pulled my world off its axis. Never before had one look done so much damage to my soul. His cutting black eyes were without empathy. He could degrade and demean with a glance. At home I had quickly become detached, always in a trance, remembering how hard I had tried to fight off his soul sucking glare.

I knew with absolute certainty that this horrible spectre could read me like a book and had the potential to hurt anyone who stood in his way. Not only was I and the investigating team in harm's way, but I knew my family were as well. I was deprived of sleep, and being exhausted I felt I didn't have the strength to protect them. He would sense this weakness, this fatigue, and use it in his evil games. He was playing with me, always planning and scheming. I was now a pawn. He had become bored with the pub, and saw me as the vessel to carry him out.

One good thing had come of it all though, Jessica was safe. Knowing that her soul and mine had bound together the night before, I was relieved to know she out of his grasp. It was a warm and comforting thought. I thanked my guides and the angels for helping me free her from reliving her own murder over and over again. In protecting her, I couldn't help but wonder if I had also protected myself. *Come on, Suzanne.* A voice of reason from my guides came to my mind. *You have to sleep... staying up all night isn't helping the situation.* I checked the time, it was 6:30am. Agreeing with my guides, I made the decision to try and rest and made my way up the stairs.

I tip-toed down the hall, passing the rooms quietly. I didn't want to wake up the kids. I could hear Alex wiggling about in his cot, he was beginning to stir and would soon realize he was in his cot alone. As I opened my bedroom door, the light from the hallway dimly lit the space just enough for me to see Mark lying on my side of the bed. *Oh bless*, I thought, *he must have been waiting up for me.* Slowly making my way towards him, I reached out to stroke his arm. He sensed my presence and jumped up with a fright.

'Sorry for making you jump,' I whispered.

'It's okay,' he gave me a weak smile.

I instantly felt his relief that it was only me who was standing at the bottom of the bed. Unsure I had the energy left to remove my boots, I began getting ready for bed. I was weak with fatigue and bone cold. When

I had finally put on my pyjamas and laid next to Mark's warm body, I could feel pains running across my upper back and shoulders. Struggling to find a comfy spot, I tossed and turned. Mark muttered from beside me, asking if I was alright.

'Yes,' I said with a tone which didn't even convince myself. I rolled over to my right and faced him, he was now wide awake.

'What time did you get home?' He pulled the pillow closer towards his head, making himself more comfortable. His tone put me on edge and the look on his face read of total disapproval.

'I got home after 4 am.'

He looked at the digital clock sitting on the dresser next to my side of the bed, confused. 'Why haven't you been to bed earlier?'

'I was too wound up Mark.'

Before either of us could settle down, Alex decided it was time to get up, his voice carrying down the hall. Mark's face fell and he let out a heavy sigh. He crawled out of bed, and threw me a glare as he headed out of the bedroom without a word. Too exhausted to deal with him at that moment, I let my body sink down into the nice warm bed, my eyes were feeling heavy. The last thing I remember was hearing his good morning greeting to Alex. I went out like a light, dead to the world.

Woken up with the sound of Mark running up the stairs, I jumped awake. He burst through the room and announced we only had twenty minutes to pick up Fran from school.

'Why didn't you wake me earlier?'

He threw me a stone faced glare, nothing more.

'Mark would it be alright if I stay here with Alex and you pick up Fran?'

His face went like thunder. 'Sure Suzanne, why not? I do every other bloody thing around here! He stomped out of the room. I dearly wished that I was still asleep and this had been just a bad dream. Still feeling groggy and with a slight nagging head-ache, I got up and went to Alex. He had fallen asleep in his buggy in front of the telly. He looked so sweet and peaceful, I left him to continue his nap. Mark, who had gone silent, quickly dressed for the cold then turned to me. He began to say something, but thought better of it and rushed out the front door.

As I walked towards the kitchen window, I could see Mark running down the road then vanishing out of view. Sitting down at the table, I noticed how dark the days were of late, and realized autumn was swiftly closing in.

REFLECTIONS

I couldn't remember the last time I had seen clear blue skies and white fluffy clouds. Trying to capture a happy occasion in my mind, I began reminiscing. I recalled days out on the beach with the kids and the dog. Those memories seemed so distant, so far away, and I longed to taste a glimpse of happy times ahead. Taking a deep breath, reality hit home. I was uncertain how long this would carry on. My stomach sank at the thought of going back to the Wheatsheaf. As I lowered my head down into my hands in desperation, the thought that this might be the death of me, crossed my mind. Assessing all the information Simon had given me the night before had left me feeling on edge. I was trying to understand the whole inexplicable situation, but it had felt too much to take in. I will never forget Simon's words as he said goodbye, "Be careful, he is dangerous! Don't fall into his trap; he wants to take your soul." Remembering how he had warned Denise to watch out for her knee, I needed to take heed of his words. We had all thought it had been an odd warning at the time, but soon after Simon and Shirley left, it became clear what he had meant. Three deafening bangs on the lounge door sent everyone into a panic. Somehow Sam managed to trip as she jumped with fright, landing on Denise's knee. It would be a long time before I forgot the look of pain on Denise's face as she was helped out to the car. We all realized we were in danger at that point. He was trying to weaken us one by one. I couldn't bear to think about it anymore and tried to block it out.

Sitting, waiting to hear Francesca and Mark coming down the street, racing each other to the front door, I took in a deep breath and tried to clear my mind. Anxious, I felt trapped, like a fairy in an hourglass. Taking note that it was the final few minutes I was going to get alone, I sat in silence meditating. Asking my guides for white light and love to lift up my spirits, I prayed they would take some of the burden off my shoulders. I knew I wasn't walking through this ordeal alone, my guides were surrounding me. It was this tiny bit of reassurance, knowing they were around me that gave me the strength to keep soldiering on. The silence was broken by Mark and Francesca arriving home

'Hi Mummy,' she said. 'It's lovely to see you.' She always seemed to say just the right thing to make me smile, 'Why didn't you come and pick me up?' she asked.

'Oh sorry, little love,' I said, as I took off her hat and the scarf that was firmly wrapped around her neck to keep off the chill, 'I've been sleeping Francesca, work kept me out late.'

'Oh sorry,' she replied with a sad facial expression. Her hair was flowing in the wind as Mark opened the door letting in a draft. He looked as red in the face as Francesca. I could tell they had been doing their usual routine, chasing each other down the street.

'Oh God,' Mark said in a gasp. 'It's freezing out there.' He closed his hands, rubbing them to bring back the circulation.

'Do you want a hot drink Mark?' I asked, trying to keep the peace.

'Yeah, I would love a coffee, has Alex woken up yet?'

'No, I haven't heard a peep from him the entire time you were gone.' Mark went into the living room and asked Francesca to be quiet as Alex was asleep. As I walked to the door, I could see her sitting at the end of the settee with her legs dangling on the edge. She looked so innocent sitting there, in a world of her own, mesmerized by the big screen.

'Come and sit down Suzanne, I will take care of the coffees,' Mark said abruptly.

I had been feeling nervous to hear what Mark had to say. I knew he wanted me to walk away from the pub, I just prayed that this conversation wouldn't lead up to a big argument. The last thing I needed right then, was another slanging match, I didn't have the energy to retaliate back or to stand my ground. He came through with a tray with the coffees and a packet of ginger biscuits and sat down at the table opposite me.

'Are you okay Mark?'

'Yeah, I am okay... it was more to ask if you are okay Suzanne?'

'I think so, I feel rundown with exhaustion and other matters, but I can handle it.'

He looked at me with sharpness in his eyes, I could tell he wasn't convinced. I could sense the tension in our conversation, and we could have cut the atmosphere with a knife. I picked up my coffee and looked into the cup asking if the milk was on ration again! Mark liked his coffee strong so he expected everyone to enjoy his 'black treacle in a cup' style of coffee making.

'Could you pass me the milk?' I asked a bit too politely.

He stood up and went to the fridge.

'Why... don't you like your coffee strong?' he asked in a sarcastic tone.

'Yes,' I said in the same tone, 'it's the highlight of my day, a real caffeine fix.' I looked at him blankly as he placed the milk on the table.

'There you go Madame,' he said as he bowed his head in an Edwardian fashion, then sat back down on the chair. He looked at me and tried to make idle chitchat, asking if I'd had a nice sleep.

'Yeah, I feel great now, I needed the rest, it's the first time in a week I have slept soundly,' I replied.

'Good, I am glad I gave you the time to rest today. Have you had a think about what you're going to do?' he asked in an inquisitive tone. I knew instantly he was talking about quitting the Wheatsheaf.

'I don't know what to do Mark, I have thought about walking away from the pub on so many occasions, it's killing me inside.' I continued the conversation, telling him how I felt and my fears about what could happen, he sat and listened to me as I broke down in front of him. He sat in the chair opposite me and reached out to hold my hand. We hadn't really had the chance to talk about my experiences, this moment had been the first real opportunity for us to discuss things.

'I want us to be strong again Suzanne,' he said. 'I can't bear to see you go through this agonising trauma every day on your own.'

I could see he wasn't finished. He then dropped the bomb.

'It hurts to see that you're not paying any attention to me and the kids. All you talk about is the Wheatsheaf constantly and it's bringing us down. It's Sam and Denise this, and Chris that... all the time.'

I was shocked to hear that Mark was losing interest in being a support for me to lean on, it was breaking my heart to know where we both stood in this mess. Realizing that I felt he no longer had my back, I began to fear he would walk away. I placed my hand on his, begging him to stay.

'Please don't leave me.'

He sunk down to the floor in front of me and placed his head on my lap. 'I am not leaving you Suzanne,' he said as the tears began racing down both our faces.

'We are a happy family, and I can't bear the thought of bringing up the kids without you.' Remembering how Mark had been such a big part of their lives. 'I will try and sort this out as soon as possible, I promise,' I said, placing my head in his hands.

We both broke down, it was an emotional moment we had both needed, to be in each other arms and to feel the bond we had built up over the years. My family are everything to me, but at that moment in time, I admit that they had taken a back seat. I was now holding onto Mark with my head on his chest, listening to his heart beat and feeling the strength of the embrace as he wrapped his arms around me to give me some much needed reassurance.

'Don't worry Suzanne, we will get through this together,' he said reassuringly. I looked into his blue eyes, his face was red with rubbing away the tears. Now I could feel a glimpse of hope. I needed Mark in my life to help pull me through this.

'I agree,' I said. 'Let's work this out together.'

'What do you mean by working this out?' he looked at me puzzled.

I let out a sigh and smiled at him. 'Well you know the situation I am in and what I am up against with Joseph, I was thinking that instead of me bottling things up and taking it out on you and the kids, why don't we try and help each other by concentrating on the family time we have? Make it more exciting when I am home. Lighten up their little lives by letting them see how happy we can be together.'

He kissed me on the cheek. 'I am happy when you're all happy, that's what makes me complete. Come on, let's go into the living room and spend some time with the kids,' he said, placing my hand in his.

Linking fingers together, I looked at Mark and thanked him for being there throughout the whole ordeal.

Mark sat on the chair opposite me, whilst I moved closer to Francesca. We both snuggled up and watched the telly. She turned to me.

'This is my favourite film Mum.' I let out a smile and nodded my head. I knew this; we must have watched this film hundreds of times in the past year.

'Really, Babe?' I said smiling down at her. 'I would never have guessed!'

As she lay with her head under my right arm, her legs curled up in a comfortable position, we were relaxing when the buggy started to move. I heard a little murmur, then a cry as the buggy wiggled a bit more. I moved closer to pop my head around to see Alex opening his eyes, his little face lit up as bright as a firework. His little legs were kicking with excitement as he held out his hands for me to pick him up and embrace him in my arms. I held him so tightly, feeling the warmth from his little body. I craved the normal maternal moments more than ever. He was moving about trying to get comfortable as I walked over to the settee.

Time soon passed by, and I glanced at the clock. It was almost 4:30pm. I had a house party in Prudhoe, booked in the diary for that night. I didn't want to leave to go to work that night, but knew I had better get a move on, as it would take me over an hour to get there.

Finally, dressed in multiple layers, I headed downstairs to say goodbye to Mark and the kids. Coming to a stop at the bottom of the stairs, I leaned against the door frame to watch Francesca. She was holding on to Alex's hands, trying to help him walk. He was a funny little boy, always laughing and blowing bubbles from his mouth; mummy's happy little soul. I loved these precious stolen moments when the kids were not aware that I was watching them. I watched their antics for several minutes and then walked into the living room and picked up Alex and hugged Francesca, kissing their little heads. Time was ticking away fast. I knew I had to leave in a couple of minutes and didn't want to be late for my house party booking. I put on my coat and said goodbye to the kids and Mark, then headed off towards the dual carriageway, signposted Blaydon, Gateshead.

The Woods

On the way to the house party, I had a lot of time to think, as the traffic was hideous at rush hour. There were red tail lights as far as I could see, all the way up the A1 in front of me. Stationary traffic was driving me up the wall, my frustration level was at boiling point.

When I finally got to the address I had been given, I was welcomed by a lovely couple, who made me feel right at home. It was so nice to chat amongst new faces, they made me feel at ease. Everyone was happy with their messages with a few of them in tears, which is a good sign for a medium! It means you have given them the information they are seeking or have given them some comfort knowing that their loved ones are still around them. As I left the house party it suddenly dawned on me how valued I felt and how lucky I am to have my gift; the ability to communicate with loved ones on the other side.

Once again, back in my car I headed back to the Wheatsheaf. I hadn't realised it was so late, 9:47pm. I had lost track of the time and was going to be late meeting the rest of the group.

Arriving at the pub, I spotted some familiar cars which were already parked up. The gang was all there. Grabbing my bag, I rushed out of the car and headed up the stone steps leading to the lounge entrance. I opened the doors and could see Sam and Denise standing at the bar.

'Hi Suzanne,' Sam said, as she came rushing over to give me a hug. 'How are you? Did you sleep well last night?'

'No, not really.'

Denise then jumped into the conversation. 'Me neither! I was climbing the walls with pain from wonder woman jumping on my best knee.' She looked at Sam, squinting her face to give her a sharp look.

I couldn't help but smile as I envisioned a full grown woman jumping on her knee in fright.

'I knew she was on the warpath all morning. I could hear her calling me from the other end of the estate!' Sam was creased with laughter.

Denise had suffered some ligament damage to the top of her knee. It was badly swollen and sore and yet here she was, ready to fight another day. 'We are all in the same boat,' she said supportively.

I was glad she had returned that night, I appreciated her support, especially as I knew she was in a lot of pain. We decided to have a chat and sort out what we wanted to accomplish with this visit to the pub.

Chris was sitting in the safe zone accompanied by a young man. He introduced his friend to me; his name was David. Placing my drink on the table I could see they had just settled down into deep conversation. He shook my hand and I instantly got a lovely warm feeling from the young man. 'Is it okay if David stays with us tonight?' The rest of the group watched so see my reaction.

'Yeah, of course he can stay, have you told him the story of the pub and what's been happening here over the past nine days?' I asked. I needed him to be prepared for any eventuality and wanted to make sure he knew how daunting the evening may turn out.

'David's a close friend of mine, we have known each other since we were kids,' he said.

I looked at the both of them and could feel they were still as close to each other than ever before.

'He is well into the paranormal side of things, he could help us with the filming and equipment if we need an extra pair of hands.'

'Great!'

They both gave me a smile, it was nice to feel the support from everyone in the group.

I discussed the previous night's events with the them. I explained that I felt there was a lot more information which we hadn't discovered yet, we had been so transfixed on the chimney breast wall and finding the little girl's remains.

'Would anyone object if we left the digging for tonight and concentrated on retracing my steps and finding out more information on the outside of the pub? Also... I would like to get a feel for how many souls are stuck outside as well as inside. I am praying to the Gods that this is going to come to a close soon, so I can go home and try and absorb what's happened to me.'

Both Sam and Denise agreed.

Chris was a bit reluctant about the idea as he had set his heart on digging, to find more evidence in the wall.

'I do know where you're coming from Chris,' I said, 'but I am very dubious about splitting the group up, as we have already witnessed that Joseph is watching our every move and I can't risk anyone getting hurt. He doesn't care who is in his way, as we have already seen in the past few days.'

'I understand Suzanne, I know it's been hard on you,' he replied.

As I looked around the group, I could feel their compassion towards me. They agreed that my idea of us all sticking together would be for the best. Secretly, I was frightened to face tonight's events. Something deep inside was firing up my instinct, I felt I needed to set up a barrier to protect myself.

'Okay Suzanne, what's the plan?' Sam spoke for the rest of the group.

'Do we need a plan?' I queried as they sat looking bewildered and confused. 'Since I walked into this pub nine days ago, nothing has ever gone according to plan. Why don't we go upstairs and check the room to see if there's any big changes, spend some time tidying up a few bricks and making the room look more presentable.'

'There's no need to tidy the room,' Chris added. 'The lads and I tidied it up before you and the rest of the group turned up.'

'Oh thank you Chris... that's helped out loads,' I let out a big sigh of relief.

'It's fine,' Chris said. He stood up, brushed past my chair and laid his hand on my shoulder to show his support, as he headed off towards the bottom of the stairs. 'I will be back in two minutes, I've left my torch in the ice room. Are we venturing outside when I come back downstairs?'

I said I thought that it was a great idea, I stood up, grabbed my bag from underneath the table and placed it over my shoulder.

Denise said because of her injury she would wait there and rest her knee. She was busy fidgeting around trying to find a comfortable position on her chair. Sam asked her if she would be alright.

'Yes, don't worry. I am fine here,' she answered.

'Okay then, if you're sure you'll be okay,' I said, grabbing a cushion off one of the benches to prop up her knee. I was really reluctant to leave Denise there, but I did understand her circumstances. It would have been too much strain for her to hobble around the grounds of the pub. I was in two minds whether to walk around outside in the cold after just recovering from a chest infection. What a picture of health we both were!

As I zipped up my coat, Sam suggested we should go out through the fire exit which was facing us, as it led straight out to the forecourt at the back. I followed Sam as she shut down the alarm and then unlocked the door. It swung open with the force of the wind. The freezing cold breeze took my breath away as I pulled my coat up to my neck and covered the bottom half of my face, leaving a gap for my eyes.

The wind was blowing a gale at the gable end, sucking in all the litter from the car park and swirling it around in the corner, next to the door. I walked towards the buildings in the grounds of the pub, trying to link into any energies which may be lurking there. Once again, I could see the cobbled floor and stables that used to be there, and pointed out the building in the forecourt. Sam was trying to keep up and take notes, as I rattled off information step by step. My attention was being pulled towards one particular tree, when a compelling vision came over me, making me gasp. As I pointed to it in the middle of the small piece of barren land, I suddenly could hear a woman crying somewhere within the woods. She was wailing in terror, her voice becoming distant with the wind, then coming louder between the gusts. At is loudest it seemed to be echoing against the thick trunks and leaves. Just as suddenly it went quiet.

'Can you hear a woman crying?'

No one answered.

The crying started faintly again as I walked closer to the end of the car park, but when I came within a few feet of the entrance to the woods, she fell silent again. I jumped over a little wall that divided the treed area from the grounds of the pub. Alone on the small parcel of land, I realized there was hardly any visibility, as the nearest light was the exterior lighting of the pub, too far to have much effect at this distance. I slowly stepped through the broken branches, it was an obstacle course of undergrowth. Just as I was about to make my way over a bit of treefall, a woman's voice whispered breathily in my ear.

'Keep up with me.'

I jumped back in terror. My blood ran cold and a sharp shiver shot down my spine. My first instinct was to run back to the pub!

'Are you okay Suzanne?' Chris shouted over to me from the entrance to the woods. As I began to turn around to answer him, I caught sight of a woman standing in the middle of the trees. She stood perfectly still, her dress flapped wildly in the wind. She wasn't of the present time, her charcoal Victorian dress spoke of an era long passed. It was torn as if she had been in a terrible struggle, her shoulders revealed where the fabric had been stripped away. The material seemed dull and soiled and dark stains marred her pinafore.

I quickly stole a glance at the others. Surely they must see her. But...

incredulously, they were all staring at me unaware of the full bodied spirit standing before us. I prayed that she would vanish before I turned back towards her and hesitated, keeping eye contact with the team. Slowly forcing myself to look back towards her, I realized to my horror, the apparition had remained. She had shifted, seeming to lean heavily to her right side, but never broke eye contact with me. It was then that she made a move. She started towards me with a hobbling gait. Unable to bear weight on her left leg, she resorted to dragging it awkwardly behind her. It was then that the unbelievable became the unconceivable. In one ungodly move, she became a blur and whooshed towards me at an inhuman rate. In the next second her face was inches from mine. I was panic struck, but managed to keep myself from backing away or running in retreat. It took every ounce of strength I had to just to keep breathing.

There were distinguishing bruises around her neck and face and what I thought was dried blood along a small unhealed gash above one of her eyebrows. Wisps of curled hair, which had once been pulled back neatly, had come loose and were whipping around her head. She noticed me staring at her wounds and began self-consciously trying to disguise the marks with her long brown hair. As quickly as she covered her neck the wind uncovered it once more. In frustration she came right up close, breathing the coldest of breaths on my cheeks. A name came to me instantly... Alice.

'He hung me from that tree, do ya hear me? Do ya know what he did to me?' She was scrunched right up against my face; her voice had gone from a sensitive cry to a threatening wailing. The smell of musty soil and rotting leaves assaulted my nostrils. I tipped my head back and stood there in shock She had no knowledge of who I was or what I was doing there, but I instantly felt she needed to tell me of the nightmare she had gone through all those years ago.

'Who hung you?' I asked.

She became very distressed and kept turning around to look over her shoulder. She was reluctant to communicate with me, seeming to still have an overwhelming fear of something or someone. Relaxing her shoulders, she pulled back from me as her face softened with sadness. I was now filled with pity for this delicate broken woman.

'I didn't say a word to George, I swear Mam, it wasn't me who squealed,' she said in a frightened voice as her body crumpled to the ground. Looking up at me, her voice distorted with pain and sadness she let out a loud cry. I noticed one of the wounds under her ear was gaping open at one end. Her neck appeared purple and bruised above the depressed markings. 'It's all gone! The shillings ain't there anymore, he took them when he got kicked out by the local folk.' As I watched Alice, she pleaded for my help to save her from the haunting memory of her past. Her spirit was trapped amongst her pain and grief. It was as if she believed they could still harm her.

'I will try and help you I said,' trying to reassure her.

She looked up to me and I was taken aback by the amount of bruising and marks around her face. Her appearance was so daunting, her lips were swollen and cracked and my eyes were once again drawn to the blackened indentations which encircled her neck. The small trickle of light from near the pub made me aware of the darkened red stains on her pinny.

'Have you seen my Patrick? she asked. 'He promised to run away with me to make a new life in Hexham.' She stood up and curled her lips into a snarl. 'He lied to me, he'd had no intention of taking me from this hell. He used me like the others!' Wailing, she placed her head in her hands, the very same hands which told their own story of how she had struggled. The backs of them were black and blue, the palms cut and scraped. Some of her fingernails had been broken off painfully short and left jagged. There were deep cuts and scratches on the backs her forearms. 'They got me to do bad things in the rooms up there.' She started to tremble at the thought of the haunting memories which were still fresh in her mind. My heart somehow reached out to Alice as she was making her confession to me. It was the information I so desperately needed, another piece to add to the puzzle.

'I knew what he was getting up to, that's why I am here in these woods.'

'What did you know?' I asked, waiting for the reply, eager to know more about Joseph, hopefully it would be something I could use against him when he attacked me again. 'What did he do?'

'Where he hid the bodies' she snapped, coming within inches of my face again. 'I can't tell you, I've told you enough!'

'No! Please don't break away like this, I need to know what happened here?' I pleaded.

She came closer to me and whispered in my ear... 'Joseph was talking to a man buddy; he told the man to move the bodies out of the roof,' she hissed.

I could tell she felt really uncomfortable, and watched as she moved her head to look at the little window at the side of the pub, the exact same one where I had spotted the little girl for the first time. Something was holding her gaze and I instinctively looked to see what she was watching.

A tall figure began to appear faintly, behind the glass. An unearthly light started to form around the entity, his wide chest and shoulders cut an imposing figure. As the glow increased, I could see it was Joseph, his piercing eyes watching us. As I turned back to look at Alice, she pulled away and in the same bizarre blur in which she had arrived, drew herself back further into the trees. I tried to follow her but, frustratingly, the undergrowth slowed me. The ground was uneven and my eyes strained to scan the ground for rocks and branches.

Arriving at the tree, I found she had vanished. I had so wanted more information from her. Standing there for a few minutes to compose myself, I let my eyes search the trees for any movement. There was nothing but barren soil and woods. Resigned to the fact she was gone I turned to re-join the team, when I noticed something that made a shiver run its course down my body. The shadow waved back and forth in front of me on the ground at my feet. I knew from where the shadow fell, its cause was somewhere above me. My soul was filled with dread, but I knew I needed to look up. Between the gusts of wind I could hear the macabre sound of rope rubbing on wood… a groaning squeak as the weight of Alice's body swayed back and forth above my head. I had never felt so helpless, as I pictured her in her last moments. Her back was turned, and as she swung the pub light softly lit her dress. It had been a dark teal blue, not charcoal, it was badly stained. The wind whipped the fabric against her naked legs. One of her leather boots was missing, her foot bare, her ankle had been snapped and assumed an awkward angle. I felt sick as I saw a dark wet trickle running down her leg from beneath her skirt. She had died in such pain at the hands of a twisted monster with no regard for human existence. I feared that all the evil that had been done to this woman had been Joseph's sick pleasure. Another gust of wind settled and I could hear twigs snapping above. With tears streaming down my face I looked up to see Alice turn her head in an unnatural fashion. There had been no breaking of twigs. Her neck clicked and snapped as she looked over to me. The crunching of vertebrae made me sick to the stomach. Part of the noose was buried within the flesh of her neck.

'Be prepared, do ya hear?' she warned, as she pointed to the window where Joseph had pressed himself against the glass. 'He will come for you!' she shouted.

It was at this moment that her eyes narrowed and her face seemed to change. In a blood curdling manner, she laughed evilly. 'What a gullible little whore you are, you think you're so fucking clever!' The penny dropped as I looked back at the window, I could see him slowly moving away from my field of vision. *Oh god! Denise is in the pub on her own and Joseph is at the top of the stairs.*

'Quick!' I screamed. 'Sam... go and help Denise, Joseph is standing at the top of the stairs, he has been watching me from the window!' I shouted.

'Oh fuck!' I could hear the panic in her voice as she ran back towards the door to the lounge. My heart was in my mouth as I quickly turned to look back over my shoulder at Alice, but this time she had vanished. Chris was stumbling through the trees to come to my rescue. As I made a step towards him, my right foot got twisted in some undergrowth and I couldn't hold my balance. I fell to the ground just as I was about to go into a sprint, my hands instinctively flew in front of me to break my fall. A sharp stinging and shooting pain came to my right hand, I must have landed on rubble. I jumped back up as quickly as I had landed on the ground, and noticed the dark wet that was beginning to ooze on my palm. I tried to analyse the wound while I was clambering back over the uneven soil, but I could hardly see anything in the dark shadows of the woods. Finally, I could feel Chris as he held his arms around me to help me with my balance. I felt relief as he guided me to the little path leading us out of the trees. We rushed through the car park and headed to the door which was open wide. We could see the light coming from within the pub. My feet barely touched the ground as I took huge strides to get to the rest of the group. They were in hot water, and God only knew what Joseph was capable of.

'Is everyone alright,' I shouted bursting through the door.

'Yeah we are fine, a bit shaken up.' Sam said with a tremble in her voice.

I was guided to a seat as the group asked me why I had panicked. It must have seemed strange for them to see me unnerved to the point of losing control. Up to that point, I had kept my own fears to myself in front of the group as much as possible.

'I will explain in a minute, I need to calm my breathing down and catch my breath!' The palm of my hand was burning, it was only a graze, but it stung and bled nonetheless.

Sadness and shock fell across their faces as I began to tell them the information I had received during my encounter with Alice, explaining that she was a very lost soul who was trapped in the woods where she had been hung.

Sam came and sat right next to me, I could see they were all interested to hear more information. I recounted what Alice had told me, Joseph and his lackeys had deceived her and set a trap to destroy her and anyone who got in their way. I told them that while Alice was talking to me in the woods, she became distracted and I looked up to the window of the toilets where I could see Joseph standing. I could see his daunting eyes glaring at me through the window. His gaze was fierce, never breaking eye contact. Then I explained how Joseph had taken over Alice and given me a sinister wakeup call about my gullibility. How I'd taken my eyes off the game. It then dawned on me that Denise was in the lounge on her own, and that's when I panicked and raised the alarm for you to run to her rescue. I told the group of the vision I had witnessed back in the courtyard days earlier, and how I had seen two men. They were both dressed in Victorian miners' clothing, One carried a small sack up the stairs, at which point I heard the other man saying, 'it will have to do for now'. I knew instantly that they were disposing of the little girl's body.

Sam was the first one to speak. 'I don't know how you are still standing Suzanne, after everything you're up against you are still managing to turn up and fight another day.'

Denise didn't hold back on the encouraging words either.

I looked at her with a smile. 'I haven't got a clue as to why I've come back to fight another day either, but I do know I made a promise to help the souls in this pub and I wouldn't be able to live with myself if I just walked away.'

Chris broke the silence with an update on the arctic room, he mentioned that Phil had accompanied him to have a look in the loft, to see if they could find any clues looking down from above the chimney breast. 'This is the exact place we are searching for remains in the wall upstairs,' he said as he drew a sketch to show us. 'Well... straight up from that point in the attic is a ledge, like a little pocket where it would have been easy to hide anything and no one would be any the wiser.

'Oh how very interesting!! That's great news.' I was hoping there was some way we might get to that part of the loft. Conferring with Chris, I asked what he thought about visiting this portion of the attic.

'No.' Chris answered my question very firmly. 'The ledge is small and someone would have to crawl over to the other side of the fireplace, to reach it. The bricks are very brittle there. As Phil and I searched more thoroughly, we noticed there were markings on the wall, as if there had previously been fires burning in the loft. We both think that the heat may have made the brickwork more fragile.'

'Are we going to take a look up there tonight?' I was keen to explore other areas, I wanted to conclude this as soon as possible.

'It's spooky up there, there is definitely something eerie about that loft.' I could tell Chris was apprehensive about us going up there.

'I think we need to go and check it out,' I said with a grin.

'If it's only going to be us, then I think the loft will hold our weight...'

'Great!' I added quickly before he had the opportunity to change his mind. I was relieved we both agreed as I felt there were more puzzle pieces to be found in the attic. Raising up from my chair, I headed up the stairs, saying to Chris that there was no time like the present to get started.

Hunger

'Oh damn it! I need to go back down stairs to get a higher chair for us to climb up.' Chris looked at me and said he would be two minutes.

I said I would wait there for him, although I didn't really feel safe being left there alone. The sound of Chris's footsteps walking back down the corridor faded away, and I immediately regretted my decision. Standing between the two rooms, I saw the kitchen was in darkness and that the room with the hole in the wall was lit only by a faint light coming from the lamp outside. My eyes were everywhere, I felt so vulnerable. I could feel a multitude of eyes watching every move I made.

With a sigh of relief, I heard Chris' footsteps coming back towards me. As I peered around the corner, I could see Sam, Denise and the rest of the group following Chris down the corridor. Denise was hobbling; I could see the pain written all over her face. We settled her on the settee, hoping to make her as comfortable as possible.

'We all stick together remember?' Sam instantly pointed out to me.'

Yes you are right Sam,' I said to her as she stood next to the fireplace, 'we are stronger as a team if we all stick together.'

'Yep... you're right there,' Denise let out a laugh, 'Can you imagine what we would have done if Joseph showed up whilst you're upstairs! I wouldn't know what to do,' she looked around as she laughed to herself which set the rest of the group laughing. Denise made a few funny comments on how she felt about being ambushed by Joseph and the rest of his followers. 'I would need an ambulance if I came face to face with him, my heart couldn't take the strain,' she said looking at me with admiration, saying the kind words, 'I don't know how you have stuck with this nightmare for so long Suzanne. Me personally, I would have bought a good pair of roller skates and skated over the hills and far away,' she laughed, sharing a dream which had been totally dependent on her knee being in better shape. The leg down to the ankle had swollen to double its size. 'I wonder if they make roller skates big enough to fit over this pig's trotter I call an ankle?'

Sam and Chris were in stitches, trying to visualise Denise's ambition to escape on roller skates. I couldn't get over how much Denise's sense of humour could lighten up everyone in the room. She managed to make those few minutes seem happy; it was very rare to see that in the kind of conditions we were under. Both her and Sam were like a comedy act when they got started. It was uplifting to see the group enjoying the lighter side of life whilst standing in a freezing cold room with the howling wind echoing through the corridor.

As I walked out of the chilly room, I noticed Chris placing a chair under the loft hatch. As he reached up and opened it, I became terrified. The sounds of children crying and the screams of women filled the empty space. *Oh I can't go in there*! My initial reaction was to shut the loft door and run out of the pub for good. Such a strange feeling came over me, one side of my brain wanted to flee and the other knew that this could reveal a big piece of the puzzle. I knew I needed to find out what was up there, even though my stomach was churning at the thought of it. *Come on then Suzanne*, I tried to convince myself, *you can do this.*

I watched Chris as he pushed himself up and then swung his leg over, bracing his foot on the end of the door frame. 'Okay,' I said, 'here goes.' Working through the swing and grabbing hold of Chris for dear life, I managed to reach out with my left hand and grab the rope. I pulled up one full tug and climbed up into the loft. After we had got our bearings, Chris looked down and said he felt the beams could take one more. It was decided that Sam would join us.

'Oh my God how unfit am I,' came Sam's voice as she struggled to get up into the loft. It was a picture seeing her jump up and grab the rope! After she found her footing, she mentioned that she had hurt her side from catching it on the door frame as she pulled herself up. 'We are all ready for the knacker's yard, fit to drop.' She smiled at me as we both looked around the loft. Sam mentioned she had come up once before, but it had terrified her. 'I didn't feel comfortable last time, it even sends shivers down my spine when I walk past this area on my way to the kitchen. There is definitely something strange about this part of the pub,' she said.

As I looked around the loft, I couldn't get over the its size and height, it was easily over eighteen feet tall in the centre. The thick oak beams were timeworn and creaked as we slowly stepped on them.

Chris led the way to the far right of the attic, shining the torch towards the chimney breast wall. As my eyes scanned around the immense empty space, an intense surge of abdominal pain took hold. Holding on to my stomach, I was besieged with the cries of so many lost souls.

Another sobering realization washed over me, souls were trapped here because they had been starved and suffocated. It was hard to pinpoint any individual spirits, scores of them filled the space. I could see women and children slumped across the walls of the loft. Some were huddled near a little fire, its flames licking up the sides of an old metal pot next to the main wall beams. I kept my vision to myself and tried to concentrate on what Chris was showing me with the torch light.

'Suzanne, if you come closer you will see what I tried to explain earlier. If you look at the bottom of the loft,' he said as he moved the light of the torch towards the far left of the chimney breast wall. 'This is the wall directly above where we are digging.' He was trying show me step by step. Once again he swung the torch towards the old beams. 'Those beams are directly above the ledge we want to be on, it would only take a child's weight to walk on the ledge and look at that side of the wall.'

'Yes, I can see it looks really frail and fragile. Is this beam and wall part of the original pub, when it was first built?' I asked.

'Yes, this side of the attic is the oldest part,' he said turning around to show me the new bricks that had been added or used as replacements over the years.

'Okay, I am satisfied that we can't attempt to crawl over the beams to get to the little ledge.' It was tucked away too neatly in the base of the wall, none of us could have reached it safely even if we had wanted to. My focus on the unattainable area was drawn away by the sight of the spirits of children, holding out their hands, begging for food. Instantly I was taken back in time. When Chris shone the light around the attic, I could see more clearly the shadows of men, some moving slowly towards to me. I could feel their cold breeze around my head and didn't want to be up there anymore; this feeling was overpowering and suffocating. Channelling through, I began seeing a vision of Joseph shouting and pushing a tearful woman down the corridor. Sensing their hatred of him and how he let them starve in the darkness, I realized this was another side to the ongoing mystery of the Wheatsheaf. I was overwhelmed by the sheer number of trapped souls. Certain there was a lot more to it. I knew in time I would work it out.

'Chris, I don't like it up here anymore, could we go back to join the rest of the group?' I asked.

'Sure Suzanne, let's get out of here, I think we've seen enough.'

Sam was the first to climb back down through the hole, first landing on the chair, I then heard her jump down to the floor. She didn't waste any time escaping the attic space. 'Okay Suzanne, I'm down.'

As I walked closer to the light from the floor below, I could see Sam and David holding on to the chair for me, directing me where to place my feet on the chair. I climbed down and felt a huge sigh of relief when my feet were firmly on the ground again. Seeing the horrors of the attic had depleted my energy, but it had been worth it. Waiting on Chris to secure the loft hatch, I took a minute to settle myself.

Sam noticed I'd gone quiet and questioned me. 'What's wrong Suzanne? I could feel you didn't like it up there.'

'There are a lot of lost souls in the attic, I could see women and children. They were surrounding me begging for food. I felt intimidated by the men in the loft who had slowly come towards me and sensed how they all hated Joseph for leaving them there to waste away in their dismal surroundings.'

'Oh My God,' Sam said, lifting her hand to her mouth. She was breathing rapidly, clearly upset.

Chris suggested we should go next door and make some hot drinks, as we all needed a break. I was relieved to feel the warmth of the kitchen, it felt totally different from the icebox of the room. I was longing to sit down to recuperate and think about what to do next. It had been frightening to see all the shadows of women and children huddled together in the corners of the loft. Seeing the cruelty lashed upon so many innocent souls made my blood curdle. They hadn't deserved to die in such a pitiless manner. *What the hell had happened here? Why did it happen? How did Joseph get away with it?*

Chris was standing next to the oven, coaxing it to light. He then filled up the old fashioned kettle with water and placed it on the hob. He grabbed a tray for me to place the cups on, and, as we waited for the kettle to boil, I decided to share my ideas with him.

'I have a suggestion.'

'What do you have in mind Suzanne?'

'While we were upstairs, I could see women and children throughout the loft, they were like shadows around the walls.'

He nodded his head in agreement, showing his understanding of what I was explaining. I found myself confiding in him often, of late.

'I knew you didn't feel safe up in the attic, how many spirits could you see up there?' He looked concerned.

'There were far too many to count, I feel they died a horrendous if not torturous death. I've been thinking... I could try and send them on to the other side, help the lost souls move on.' Their plight had saddened me.

'Okay,' he said in an edgy manner, saying he was happy to go with whatever I felt was best.

The Mist

I felt the break was well earned after what I had witnessed in the attic. Chris told everyone about my plan to send on the lost souls from their lofty prison. Denise asked if they had been trapped for all those long years, to which I answered that I thought that they had. They had been too frightened to venture out. I also told her I could feel their pain and hunger hitting the bottom of my stomach. I think the group were surprised that I could feel the pain of those poor souls, but mediums can and often feel different sensations depending on the situation they are in at the time.

When we had finished our break, I suggested we make an area in the centre of the room to use for sending on the souls. I asked Chris if I could have some salt from the kitchen to make a circle of protection. Sam and Denise asked if they could film me and I agreed. They found themselves a comfy spot on the couch, wrapping themselves up, as the temperature was dropping. It was hard to stay in that room for long periods of time, it was so cold. I asked Stephen, Chris and David to stand within the circle of salt I had marked out in the middle of the floor. Chris stood to my left and Stephen was to my right.

'Now everyone, close your eyes, and then take one step forward for protection.' I was standing at the top of the circle looking around, seeing everyone was safe in the room before I closed my eyes. I requested the group to clear their minds from anything that would prevent them from feeling the presence of my spirit guides. 'I ask for the Angels' hierarchy to come and release the lost souls in this pub,' I called out, taking deep breaths, breathing in through my nose and out through my mouth. I relaxed my shoulders and took in the love and light from the Angels.

In deep meditation, I began to see through my psychic eye. I connected to my guides and began to clear my mind. I was repeating our Lord's prayer in my head. This helps to connect to higher Angels, as I ask for their protection. As I continued, I began to see little blue and purple lights flickering in my psychic eye and felt it was time to begin sending on the lost souls. I quickly glanced around the room, everyone was standing in the circle feeling relaxed. Sensing we were not alone, I could feel there were spirits connecting to the séance circle. As I closed my eyes, my spirit guides told me it was time to call out for the lost souls and send them on to the other side.

'Come into the circle, don't be afraid, follow the light towards me.' Channelling through, there was an instant feeling of pressure, like a heavy weight was pressing down on the top of my head. This feeling made it hard to relax and distracted me from moving the souls into the light. Hearing the voices of children softly echoing around the room, I could feel an intense energy growing. My heartbeat was drumming in my ears. I could see spirits, which seemed to be walking down stairs that weren't visible to me. A man began calling out as he moved towards me. He told me he was called Bill and that he had fallen down some cellar steps and broken his neck. As I channelled through to him, I felt he looked to be in his 50's. He wore a double breasted tweed suit with cuffs at the ankles of his trousers, popular in the 1940's. A neatly folded handkerchief of paisley silk showed its corners in his breast pocket and matched his long tie. I was struck by the neatness of his apparel in contrast to his confused facial expressions. The poor soul, couldn't understand how or why he had been stuck in the pub since falling into the cellar, dying instantly.

As the channelling continued, I began to feel as if I was being bombarded by the numerous souls that had been trapped up in the loft. They seemed to be coming at me from all angles. My heart went out to the crying children, as they didn't understand what was going on at all. They were so confused, all I could do for them was tell them to follow the light in the centre of the circle.

I asked my guides to call upon the higher Angels to help remove the souls from the loft. I could feel my hands being lifted up and my outstretched hands and fingers formed a triangle, the symbol of higher Angels.

'I ask for their loved ones to come and help the souls to move on and find peace in heaven,' I called out. As the words left my lips, I could feel a tingling feeling in the centre of my hands as I joined them together. It was time to gently urge them on. 'Go and join your families, embrace your reunion in the gates of heaven.' I could feel the room changing. With my eyes still closed, I continued meditating and could see the lights becoming clearer and more vibrant.

'Oh my God, Suzanne,' Sam said. I quickly turned my head and opened my eyes and looked directly to where Sam was standing next to Denise. They looked like they had seen a ghost. I was annoyed with the interruption, the lights from the ceiling were blinding and it had broken my concentration away from releasing the souls.

As the minutes passed, I felt the room was lifting, the tension lessening. Taking a deep breath, I asked the three to take a step back from the circle, as the visual was about to close and I needed to protect them after having participated in the visual. My energy level had been drained from the experience, the life sapped out of me. I was feeling faint and dizzy. I needed to sit down and take a minute to recuperate.

'Suzanne, are you okay?' Sam asked as she walked over to me. 'I am really sorry for interrupting you earlier, I was in shock, you didn't see what Denise and I could see,' she said excitedly.

'What do you mean?' Sam had the camcorder in her hand.

'Watch and see for yourself!' She rewound the camcorder with trembling hands, eager to show me what they'd caught on film. She pressed play. 'Now watch when you put your hands in the air, the ceiling lights behind you,'.

'Okay.' I leaned back in my chair and listened to my voice coming through the little speaker on the side and watched the screen. When I got to the part where I reached my hands in the air, I could see a mist faintly coming from the light shades. It was indistinct at first, but when I asked the souls to go into the light, opaque white mist began billowing from the ceiling. At that point I could hear Sam's astonished voice on the recording. 'That's unreal!' I handed the camcorder over to Sam, she stood up and began to show the others the footage. I sat in shock, listening to everyone's comments.

'Oh I can't believe what I am seeing. This is amazing. Suzanne you could lecture from this footage, it's unbelievable how the mist is billowing out of the lights.' I was sitting and listening to all the comments and trying to find my breath. The atmosphere still felt intense and highly charged. After everyone had calmed down we decided to call it a night. I packed my gear into my bag, and we all went downstairs together.

When we reached the bottom of the stairs, I automatically looked around to Joseph's corner and could see a figure standing in the middle of the room. It was Joseph. He had the ability to look straight through me. His face was set in anger from knowing that I had freed the souls that he had controlled for decades. His lips turned up into a snarl and the veins in his temples stood up like a roadmap to hell. Infuriated with my accomplishments, he knew I had stripped him of his domination over the souls in the attic. They were free. With a growl edging towards a roar, he charged towards me. 'How fucking dare you meddle in my affairs! I am coming for you bitch...You will feel my wrath. If it's the last thing I do, I WILL destroy you!' he screamed in temper.

All I could do was stand my ground and pray he would go away, as I didn't have any energy left to face him. I was thoroughly frightened, and I knew without doubt that he could sense my fear. A slow evil grin formed on his face to confirm he had noticed.

'Are you alright Suzanne?' Chris broke my attention away.

'Yes,' I said as I spun my head around to see his kind face looking back at me. I quickly turned back to face my nemesis who was waiting to blow me into oblivion and beyond, but his energy had vanished. What a relief that was. Joseph had made his threats painfully clear. I didn't want to stay in the pub any longer than I needed to, but I didn't have the heart to say I had just been threatened by Joseph again. I wanted to make sure everyone went home buzzing, having seen the concrete evidence of the mist coming out of the ceiling lights. I could hear the group all talking about what had happened upstairs, they were excited and it didn't seem fair to put a damper on their good mood. We all made arrangements to meet back up again the next night and said our goodbyes.

Abandonment

Driving home, my mind was racing a hundred miles an hour, and yet, I was aware of a foreboding silence echoing around the car. It was as if my weary body was trying to absorb the stifling heaviness around me. I looked forward to seeing the familiar landmarks of home and tried to keep my horrid thoughts of the Wheatsheaf at bay for the remainder of the journey.

My chest felt heavy after inhaling an enormous amount of dust over the space of a couple of hours. Even parking the car was a strain, my shoulders were aching and my neck felt stiff. Taking a couple of minutes to compose myself, I found it impossible to stop my mind from reflecting back. Haunting images were roiling deep within me and I was beginning to feel a strange pressure burning inside my soul. I completely fell apart.

I was drowning in my own trauma, fear had become my best friend. *'What am I going to do?'* I asked aloud in the silence of the car. *'Have I bitten off more than I can chew?'* I placed my head in my hands and could feel a lump in my throat, I struggled to hold back the tears. My body began to tremble. With my fingers embedded in my hair and tears streaming down my face, I tried to force my breathing to slow down, to help gain my composure. It was impossible. The shock from the Wheatsheaf's nasty events rushed around my aching body. I couldn't look into the rear view mirror for fear of seeing my haunted reflection looking back at me.

After a few minutes had passed, I managed to take a few deep breaths and then slowly raised my head. 'Go home,' a voice came fresh in my mind, 'Suzanne you're exhausted.' I gathered up my belongings and headed for the front door. The brisk September morning breeze cut through me like a thousand knives. My chest became tight as I pulled down the front door handle and stepped into the hall.

I jumped back in fright as the living room light flashed on. *'Oh no... Marks still up.'* I opened the living room door to see him standing two feet in front of me.

'What time do you call this?' He said in an abrupt tone.

'I am sorry Mark I didn't realize the time.' I timidly walked closer to greet him with a hug.

'Don't bother!' he snapped as he brushed past me and nearly knocked me off my feet. I was stunned at his reaction.

'This is a lovely welcome home,' I muttered under my breath.

'What's the matter with you?' I asked in a firm tone. My body was in desperate need to sit down. The exhaustion I was feeling made me feel frail and weak. I let out a long sigh. The last thing I needed at that moment, was a confrontation with Mark. I could clearly see he was upset and knew without a shadow of a doubt, that this was far from over. He sat down in the armchair opposite me, his anger hanging, an awkward atmosphere between us.

'Do you know what you're putting me through Suzanne?' he said, like a father talking down to a naughty child.

As soon as I heard the domineering tone in his voice, my guard shot straight up. 'What the hell is wrong with you?' I hissed, glaring in his direction.

'Look Suzanne, I don't want to give you a hard time, but this situation makes me absolutely furious. You don't even bother ringing me to let me know you're okay! I worry so much about your wellbeing, especially when you have that evil ghost attacking you every minute of the day.'

I let out a small laugh to myself as I shook my head. I wished Mark could have seen how difficult it was to walk out the door of my cozy home every night, while trying to find the strength to face my nemesis in that dreaded pub. Maybe then Mark could have shown some compassion toward me through this ordeal. But sadly I knew he didn't see it and suspected he never would.

'It wasn't my plan to go through this Mark!' I yelled. I could feel my throat tightening as the last words left my lips.

'I know you're struggling with your own personal hell Suzanne. It's written all over your face, every time I clap eyes on you I can feel the strain you're under.' He was wringing his hands together in utter frustration. 'I don't know what to do for the best,' he growled. With his fury, I could see the veins were bulging out of his neck alarmingly. We had, like any normal couple, our ups and downs, but this was scaring me. I had never seen Mark so angry before that point. I didn't look at him as he shot up out of the chair and walked out of the room. Banging noises began coming from the kitchen.

'What are you doing?' I shouted.

'Nothing!!' he shot back. I could see his reflection through the glass dining room door. He was anxiously pacing up and down, trying with all his might to calm himself down. I slowly pulled myself up from the settee to see him now standing directly in front of me. 'Sorry for shouting,' he said as he bowed his head and looked at the floor.

'It's ok.' I stepped closer to him and rubbed his arm with a reassuring delicate touch then walked past him towards the kitchen. Grabbing a glass off the bench, I stood near the sink taking in gulps of water to quench my thirst, trying to settle the tightness in my throat. I tapped the switch on the kettle having decided I was in desperate need of a hot toddy to relax me. This was a good chance to distance myself from Mark for a few minutes; hopefully the dust would settle. *I can't be bothered.* I'd had one hell of a night and knew no matter how exasperating or painful, there was no other choice but to walk back into the living room and face the music.

Sitting back down, I noticed Mark was sitting on the chair opposite me, and there was no way on earth that I could miss the look on his face. Obviously my earlier delicate touch had been futile, he wasn't convinced. *Oh God, this conversation is going to be a bundle of laughs.*

I didn't utter a word. Sitting in silence, holding on to my drink tightly, I waited with a strange mix of eagerness and foreboding to hear what Mark would have to say.

He looked at me with sadness in his eyes as he took a deep breath. 'Suzanne I've had enough.'

I looked straight at him in shock. Looking back, I am unsure which saddened me more, the words he had just uttered or the tone with which they had been spoken. 'What do you mean… you've had enough?' I overly stressed the you've. 'Enough of what exactly?

'Well… you know exactly what. The Wheatsheaf of course. It's becoming an addiction with you. You've completely pulled our relationship to shreds. You've ignored me and worse… you've ignored the kids. I refuse to watch this happening every bloody day… I can't take it anymore. I am going to take some time out. My brother Paul is coming over in the morning around 8 a.m. He has suggested I stay with him for a couple of nights to sort myself out. I am sorry Suzanne, but…'

'Right!' I shouted at him to stop talking. 'Let's get this straight. So you're walking out on me… and the kids? So…in my hour of need you're turning your back on me? You haven't got a fucking clue what I'm going through, nor do you give a shit.' I knew deep down Mark had made a few valid points, but at that moment, I wasn't about to admit it. My anger raged and my reaction was shameful, I screamed from the top of my lungs and punched my fist through the air. The look on Mark's face was a mixture of fear and shock as he grabbed a hold of me.

'Calm down Suzanne! Please calm down!' He pulled me towards him so tightly I could hear his heartbeat pounding in his chest. That's when reality hit home.

'What am I doing?' I asked, as I took a deep breath and pulled away from Mark. 'Sorry,' I said, as I sat back down wiping away my tears with frustration. Weeping seemed such a betrayal to my anger.

'What the hell is wrong with you Suzanne? You're acting like a mad woman possessed!'

I slumped back down on the settee, my head was pounding with rage. Having trouble comprehending what I was hearing from Mark, I needed time to get my head around the past few minutes. This had become an ordeal. Awkward silence once again hung in the air. His silence fueled my rage even further, cracking me up inside. I was furious at the thought he could even imagine walking out on me at a time like this.

As the minutes passed, it quickly became time to wake up Fran. Real life wasted no time in reminding me that things moved on whether we wanted them to or not. Mark finally broke his silence and said he would get her ready for school.

'Don't!' I said, shooting up from the settee. 'I will wake her up!' Turning around, I faced him as he stood there like a lost child being told off. I went right up to his face and glared at him and hissed 'You'd better get some clothes packed if you're leaving by 8 o'clock.!' Walking up to the top of the landing, I could feel my breathing becoming tighter and wanted to collapse in a heap on the floor. Holding on to the top banister as if my life depended on it, I was adamant to see this day through, with or without Mark's help.

As I walked into Francesca's room, I could see her little blonde head peeking out of the quilt. She looked so peaceful I didn't want to wake her. Slowly, I made my way to the top of her bed and began to stroke her hair. 'Come on little love,' I said in a hushed tone. She began to stir. Her little head pulled away from the quilt. 'Come on it's time for school.'

'Ok Mummy,' she said whilst letting out a yawn.

I couldn't stay in her bedroom a moment longer; Alex was waking up. He was blabbering away to himself. Opening the door, I peeked through to see Alex standing at the end of his cot with a cheeky smile on his face. He started to gurgle and laugh as I carried him down the stairs and into the living room. Mark was busying himself with packing some clothes into a carrier bag. He briefly looked at me, long enough that I noticed he had been crying, his red eyes gave the game away. Alex was excited to see his Dad as he stretched his little arms out for him.

Do you think you could possibly pull yourself away from your packing to pull out his high chair from the dining room please?' I said snidely and without eye contact. I couldn't look Mark in the face knowing he was adamant in walking out on us. For a brief while, everything fell into a normal morning routine. My heart sank when the doorbell rang. Mark went to answer it, then stopped and looked at me.

'That will be our Paul... I will ask to him to wait outside for a couple of minutes?' He muttered more to form a question than a statement.

'If you want to,' I replied holding a tight rein on my emotion. *Don't let the kids see us upset Suzanne.* I could hear them talking at the front door, when Francesca came barging into the room.

'Mum why is Uncle Paul at the front door?' She looked at me with fear on her face.

I had hoped she hadn't heard them talking. I'm sure she had picked up on the stress in the air. 'Francesca your Dad's going away for a couple of days,' I said as I grabbed hold of her hand.

'WHAT?? NO!!' She screamed and pulled her hand away from me and quickly ran to the front door. Her sobbing echoed down the hallway. 'Please Daddy... don't go,' she pleaded. She became hysterical.

I had never seen her this upset before and couldn't do anything but sit there and listen to my daughter's heart breaking as she crouched at her father's feet begging him to stay.

'Mark!' I shouted as he walked through into the living room with Francesca in his arms. She was gripping on to his neck for dear life and sobbing her little heart out. I was now breaking down myself. The feeling of abandonment was rife. *Can he not see how much I need him to keep the family safe?* He sat Francesca down on the settee next to me and knelt in front of her.

'Listen,' he said with his voice breaking. 'Daddy's going away for a little while.'

I then watched as they held each other in the tightest of embraces. Helplessly, all I could do was watch as my family was crumbling away piece by piece before me.

Francesca was hysterical as Mark stood up. He looked at me with sorrow in his eyes. 'I've got to go,' his voice was broken.

He picked up his bag, then gave the kids a kiss.

'Please change your mind Mark,' I pleaded as he walked towards the hall.

He looked at me and gave me a broken smile. 'I will give you a ring later on today… I promise.' And…with that, he turned and walked out.

The house felt cold. I stood motionless, staring at the front door, expecting him to have a change of heart and come back in with open arms.

Seconds turned into minutes. I was dumbfounded. My concentration span was sporadic. Every time I tried to grasp what had happened, my train of thought would falter, my mind would go blank. All I could see in my mind's eye was Mark's face, standing there, a broken man who had walked out on his broken family.

'Why? Why has he gone?' Francesca was curled up in a ball on the floor.

'Come here love.' I opened my arms inviting my little girl to come and nestle into me.

'No!' she shouted from the top of her lungs, at which point she jumped up from the floor and ran out of the room.

'Francesca,' I shouted. 'Please come here so I can explain.'

'No!' she shouted. 'I hate you! I hate you!'

I stood up from the chair and slowly walked towards the hall. She was curled up in a ball in the middle of the stairs, her head nestled down resting on her lap.

'Come on,' I gently pleaded. 'Francesca please…'

'No!' She looked at me with hatred written all over her face. 'You did this!' she yelled as she stood up and hissed at me. 'It's all your fault. Now my dad's gone away.'

'I am sorry Francesca. For everything.' I began to break down. We were both in hysterical tears. She quickly ran up the stairs.

'I'm going to school!' she shouted.

'Come on love, you can't go to school this upset.' I slowly made my way up the stairs and could hear her moving around in her room. 'Please Francesca… come to me, we can talk it through. As I opened the door, she was rifling through her drawers to dress for school. She didn't look up.

'Go away… leave me alone.'

'Okay. But listen to me, I didn't want your dad to leave today. It's

ABANDONMENT

hard on us all. I am sorry you hate me Francesca. I never wanted to hurt you.' Tears once again streamed down my face.

I realized she needed a little time to calm down. As I turned to walk out of the door, I felt a cold shiver running down my spine which stopped me in my tracks. I was taken completely by surprise. Feeling an oppressive evil circulating around us, my fear began penetrating through my bloodstream. I felt sick to my stomach and began trying to take deep breaths.

'Mum what's wrong?' Her little voice broke my concentration.

'I need to sit down.' I slowly made my way down the stairs towards the living room. Alex was happy and content sitting on the floor playing with his toys. I slumped down on the chair with Francesca only seconds behind me. Glancing at the clock, and seeing it was already 8:50, I exhaled with exhaustion.

'Why don't we have a day off?' I said to her with as much enthusiasm as I could muster, to try and lighten the moment. I could see she wasn't in any state to go to school and I was in no frame of mind to face the outside world. Trying to drown out what I had experienced upstairs, I attempted to put on a brave face and leave the digestion of what had happened until I had free time to sit and think.

The morning flew by. I had no energy left by 1 p.m., my eyelids seemed to be hitting the floor. With Fran watching her movie, I tucked Alex in beside me, wrapping a blanket around us. We laid down on the settee, warm and cozy and with much needed calm, I drifted off to sleep.

'Suzanne wake up!' A man's gruff voice whispered in my ear. My eyes flew open. The living room was in total darkness. Panic struck me as I looked around and realized I was alone. 'Oh my God!' I screamed out loud, my head full of terrifying possibilities. 'Where are the kids?'

Weak light from the street filtered in, barely illuminating the clock. 9.30 p.m. *What? That can't be the right time! Oh no... where have the past eight hours gone to?* I raced for the light switch, and felt a chilling disappointment when it failed to light. Before I could gather my thoughts, I heard something which made my blood run cold. The sound of children's laughter was coming from the top landing. Creepy maniacal laughter, the laugher of more than one child. I let out a scream of fright.

My heart stopped beating at the sound of footsteps running up and down the corridor. The resonance of the footsteps gave away their location. In and out of bedrooms, then back to the hall. All the while the laughter continued, interspersed with whispered conversations which seemed just out of earshot. There are no words to describe the fear I felt for the children and myself. I felt frozen to the spot. Unable to think straight, I tried to quickly calm myself and figure out my next move. The words, *what am I going to do*, ran like a recording on a loop in my brain. All I wanted was to hold both my children in my arms to keep them safe from harm.

As quickly as the laughter had begun, it ended. A deadly silence swept rapidly around the house. Standing in the hallway and looking up the stairs, I waited anxiously. My instincts were on full alert, both listening and watching out for any sudden movements. Suddenly, a white mist appeared at the top of the stairs. It seemed to glow and churn within itself like a rolling thundercloud. Hovering on the top step, it seemed to be building up in intensity. I gasped as it suddenly started to move from step to step, down toward me. Picking up speed, it headed in my direction. A cold breeze rushed from the floor and up my legs. It wasted no time in enveloping me and entering my mouth with each breath I took. Pain shot down my throat, as if the air itself was on fire. I was terrified. Frozen to the spot and unable to move, I screamed. I couldn't stop my body from trembling inside, I tried to focus my thoughts. *Oh God please help me.* I prayed this evil would vanish as quick as it appeared. Fearing for the children, I wanted to fly up the stairs, but was incapable of movement. My eyes were firmly fixed on the top of the landing where I needed to be.

Suddenly a voice which I instantly recognized, broke the ominous silence. *That's Francesca's voice.* Her laughter sent shivers down my spine. I could hear her chatting away as though she was talking to someone I couldn't see. Faint whispers echoed down the stairs. I could see her little blonde head as she appeared at the top landing. *Francesca!!* I shouted. No words from my lips were spoken out loud. I was trying to catch my daughter's attention, nothing was working, it was futile. I was obviously invisible to her.

Helplessly, I watched her methodically take the stairs one at a time down the first few steps and then stop. I could see her turn, looking up towards her bedroom smiling and giggling to herself. *Who is she talking too?* I screamed within myself. Frustrated and petrified, I shook with the strain of trying to unstick myself from my stationary state. An unseen force was pinning me down. Struggling with all my might to break free, I watched as she began to walk back up the stairs towards the bedrooms. Nearing the top, she turned and looked at me with a horrid, subdued expression on her face. It was as if she was looking at me through another's eyes. I was shocked. *This isn't Francesca. I began wracking my brains. Why is she behaving this way?* Her eyes looked unnaturally fierce as she glared at me. Her pupils dark and menacing. Petrified inside and anticipating what would happen next, I didn't have to wait long to find out.

'Hello Mummy,' she spoke in a sarcastic tone. She pulled her head back laughing, I was instinctively sure that it had been a man's voice coming through my daughter. 'You bitch!' she yelled, holding on to the banister as she ran halfway down the stairs.

Aggressively, she began hissing, as foul words exploded from her mouth. My heart broke on hearing the perverse language coming from my innocent child. Her face seemed to twist and contort as she started again. 'I am coming for your soul!' she spat at me. 'You think you're so fucking clever little girl!' she turned around and bounded up the stairs. An almighty bang resonated through the house as she slammed her bedroom door shut. The fear of God swept over me.

'Francesca!!!' I screamed a silent scream from the top of my burning lungs. An empowering rage inside my soul began to course through my veins. *That's it!* I thought. *I've had enough.* Pushing with all my might, trying to break free, a voice came into my mind. 'Come on Suzanne! Push yourself…push yourself free NOW!!'

The energy began to weaken and my lifeless body collapsed to the floor. My muscles felt on fire from straining against being paralyzed for so long. I felt overwhelmed with relief. Finally, the spell was broken.

Filled with adrenaline and fear for the children, I ascended the stairs two at a time, like a woman possessed. Pausing for a moment whilst standing outside the bedroom door, I took in a long deep breath to ready myself for what was inside. My hand went for the door handle. 'Oh God, it's freezing cold,' I gasped. *Who is behind this door with my children?*

Fearfully, I realized I already knew. I tried turning the handle in both directions. It wouldn't budge. I rattled and shook the handle, pushing on the door in a blind panic. The entire time I was trying to force the door open, I was shouting her name over and over again until my voice became hoarse.

'What's that smell? Fuck!!' Smoke began curling out from under the door. Its wisps seemed to reach out and grab my legs then climb up to assault my nostrils. It seemed just when I'd met the worst fear I'd ever felt, someone moved the bar.

'FRANCESCA!!! PLEASE OPEN THE DOOR!!' Screaming out for

my daughter, sobbing, I continuously banged frenziedly on the unbudging wood. I was beyond furious. *This is not real!! I am going to wake up any moment now!!* Now fearing the worst, my heart fracturing into a million pieces, I prayed harder than I had ever done.

'MUMMY!' Strangely, hearing my daughters screams of terror sent a feeling of hope. It was a tiny breakthrough. My daughter was calling out my name.

'Thank God, she is calling for me!'

'MUMMY THERE'S A FIRE!!!' Her screams were echoing around the room. Relief and hope had been fickle visitors, washed away as quickly as they had come. Once again, I was hysterical; horrific scenarios began flashing in my mind's eye. *What the hell was I going to do?* Mustering up what I felt was maybe the last of my strength, I decided to try and barge through the bedroom door once more. I braced myself and, as I threw all of my body weight against it, it suddenly gave way.

Francesca stood with her back to the wall, pointing and screaming. I was struck by how tiny and vulnerable she looked. Then it dawned on me, *where the hell was Alex?*

'Francesca where's Alex?' I shouted with panic in my voice.

Unable to divert her gaze from the flames, she blurted out, 'I don't know Mummy!!'

Overtaken with motherly instinct, I shouted to her, 'Francesca come to me!!! Run into my arms!!'

She seemed frozen to the spot, her body wracked with choking coughs.

'Run NOW!'

Thick black smoke circulated around us, reminding me we had very little time.

'FRANCESCA…NOW!!!'

She broke her gaze from the flames and looked over to me and broke into a run.

As I bent down to scoop her up, I watched her little body collide into mine. We briefly hugged with relief as I quickly moved her out of harm's way into the hall. Running back in and whipping the throw from the end of the bed, I moved towards the flames preparing to tackle the fire. Overcome by the acrid smoke, my lungs burning, I was coughing uncontrollably. Spreading the throw quickly over the flickering blaze, the room grew dark as the last embers were smothered. Back in darkness and still surrounded by thick smoke, I rushed back to Francesca and hugged her tightly. 'Sweetheart, you need to stay right here while I look for Alex!'

'No, Mummy! Don't leave me!!' She became hysterical.

'Are you sure you don't know where Alex is?'

'No!' she exclaimed through her tears. 'All I remember was sitting watching the telly. Then I woke up and saw the flames in my bedroom.'

With Francesca in tow, I quickly moved across the room and opened the window. A bit of light from the street managed its way into the room.

'What's happening Mum? Why was there a fire in my bedroom?' She wiped away her tears between bouts of coughing.

I was unable to answer, focused now on finding Alex. With Francesca tight at my side, we slowly went down the dark hall towards Alex's bedroom. Opening the door slowly, afraid of what I might find, we found him sound asleep in his cot, oblivious to the situation he had been in. His little legs hanging out between the bars. Tears of relief trickled down my cheek. Thank God!! We quietly left the room and let him sleep.

Nearing Francesca's room, we came to a stop in the doorway. Upset, she grabbed me by the waist and buried her head as close as physically possible beside me. Her little body was shaking with shock. I stroked her hair, trying my best to calm her down. Once again I felt her stiffen. 'Mum?' she asked, stopping to cough. In a trembling voice she continued, 'Is that my favorite book on the floor?'

'Stay here love, I need to go take a look.'

She was reluctant to let me go.

'It's OK darling. I will be just a few feet away.' Making my way slowly towards the floor at the end of the bed, I began to make out the corner of a book cover, its edges burnt and the colour distorted. Lifting a corner of the throw, I could see the burned pages of a book, still in fragile book shape within the ashes. The carpet was melted and scorched but more alarmingly, the edges of the bedding had nearly caught. Looking closer I noticed the comforter edges were blackened where the flames had licked up the edge of the bed and the sliver paint of the bed frame had bubbled and blistered.

Our eyes met as it dawned on me. *Thank you God for your protection! This could have burnt the house down to the ground and us with it.* I was grateful also that Francesca had no recollection of what happened there that night. However, it also served to confirm my worst fear. Joseph's dark evil had entered our home. As a family, we had now become victims.

'Come on little love,' I said sullenly, as we walked towards the landing. I was finding it difficult to breath, my body was on its last threads of energy. We sat down in darkness on the top stair, I couldn't absorb what had happened.

'MUM?' Francesca broke my trance as she sat beside me. As I wrapped my arm around her I pulled her close and we both wept. My head was pounding with the strain.

'It's going to be OK,' I said weakly, trying to convince myself as much as her. I looked into her eyes, and in the dark I could just make out my daughter looking back into mine. *Oh God help us.*

'What's happening?' she asked as she held her head in her little hands and cried her heart out.

'I don't know love, but I do know one thing, I am ringing your Dad. I placed my hands over my mouth to stop my frustration from lurching out of my body. The last thing I wanted was an outbreak of fury, my daughter had seen enough that night. I was dumbfounded how Alex had slept through all the commotion. It was beyond me, but maybe it had been a blessing in disguise. Although the flames had been put out, there was still one burning question, *how did he end up sleeping in his cot? This can't be.* 'Did you put Alex to bed Francesca?' She looked at me confused and blurted out a no.

'It's OK.' I gave her a comforting smile as I masked over the few seconds of renewed panic. *There must be an angel watching over me after all.* Looking down at Francesca, it was written all over her face, we had both just experienced a traumatic ordeal. 'Little Miss... I think we both deserve a hot chocolate and... I think a movie and a cuddle on the sofa are in order.' I had hoped the comfort would let her drift off for some much needed sleep.

'Okay,' she replied timidly. As I watched her taking her time down the stairs, a notion of dread penetrated through me. I was now concerned for my family. Entering the living room, I headed for the lamp, praying that it would come on this time. I desperately needed to fill the house with light. As the light chased away the darkness, I sighed with relief.

In trying to sort through what had happened, nothing made sense. Thankfully Francesca drifted off quite quickly, leaving me to watch her favourite movie. My head was bouncing with images of the house burning and Francesca caught amongst the flames. *For God's sake, please let me find some solitude.* The movie came to its end without me watching a bit of it. I tried to shut off and doze, but it was to no avail. Then it dawned on me, Mark... ring Mark. I wrestled with the notion of calling him, given the chilliness between us. I gently wriggled away from Francesca without waking her and grabbed my phone. Seconds felt like hours as the ring tone went unanswered.

'Hello,' came a groaning voice at the end of the phone.

'Mark it's me.'

'Suzanne it's 3am., why aren't you asleep?'

'I can't sleep, I am frightened Mark, we have had one hell of a night. Please come home in the morning? We really need to talk.'

'Okay… now can I get some sleep?' I wasn't sure he had absorbed a word I had said.

We agreed to meet up at 10 o'clock. *Why didn't I tell him what had happened? Would he have thought it was just a sympathy ploy to bring him running back?* Feeling deflated, I sat with my head hung down and stared at the floor. I honestly didn't know if I could make it until morning. Petrified, I sat in deadly silence and looked over to see Francesca sleeping peacefully where I'd left her. I glanced at the clock, it was now 4 a.m. and I decided to snuggle beside her on the sofa. Worried about Alex in his room I slept restlessly. I needed one eye open.

Alex's screaming from the top of his lungs woke me with a start. I shot up from the couch and raced up the stairs, still half asleep. My body desperately wanted to lie back down, I was aching from head to toe.

I went through the motions of changing Alex and carrying him downstairs on autopilot. There was a feeling of dread throughout the house. My suspicions left me feeling that the morning would be filled with chaos, I could feel it in the air. Checking the time, 9:10, brought both a feeling of relief and nervousness that Mark would soon be there. I hoped he would truly listen when I explained everything that had happened. I placed Alex in his highchair in the living room, needing us all to be together. I couldn't relax, frightened of what would happen next. Even leaving the kids alone for one second made my blood run cold.

Intruder

I jumped when I heard a knock at the door, my nerves were jangled. Glancing down the hall, I could see an image of a man through the privacy glass. He was about to pull down on the door handle. Quickly, I ran down the hall, turned the key and opened the door. I could see Paul's car driving off, Mark turned and waved to him.

'Hi,' I said meekly. I felt nervous and unsure as I let him in, unable to hold eye contact and busied myself with closing and locking the door. He mumbled a hello as he walked into the living room and fully embraced the welcome from the kids, especially Francesca, who wouldn't leave his side.

I was very distant towards Mark at first, not knowing what to say. Seeing the love between him and the kids, I decided to wait before talking with him. My kids are more important, the time spent embracing their father's love should be theirs to cherish.

As time went on, and we all settled in, the day moulded into fun and laughter. It was what I needed more than anything else. I would have loved to be in someone else's shoes at that time, just to experience normality. It's a blessing to see your life as your own making. But, accepting reality, I realized that, at that vulnerable moment in time, I feared for my own life.

We settled down to a movie, finishing off a lovely day. The kids seemed more settled under Mark's calming influence. The house felt different, calmer as well and I began to relax a bit more. I asked him if we could talk after the kids went to bed, and remembered how relieved I felt when he looked at me and smiled.

'Yeah of course we can.' He gently held my hand then pulled me towards him. His embrace felt electric. I was in desperate need of being held, to have someone help take the pain away. Mark has a good heart and I knew he would never intentionally hurt me. But with what we had experienced, I could see his point of view. Fully understanding this, I realized that it must have been damned hard for him to return home that morning.

I went to get a blanket from upstairs as Francesca insisted she wasn't going to sleep in her room that night for fear of what happened a mere twenty-four hours earlier. She was scared to death and tearful of the thought of going back up there. She feared that whatever had created the fire may rear its ugly head once more. I didn't argue with her, deep down I harboured the same fears. Her room was still in no fit state either, evidence of the fire was evident there and the stench of smoke still hung in the air. Her little face showed such relief when I tucked the blanket around her on the sofa.

As the kids settled down, Mark suggested we talk in the dining room, out of the way of 'little ears' lying on the couch. Pulling up a chair opposite him, I began thrashing things out with him and suggested we try a little harder in some parts of our relationship. The conversation grew deeper as we delved into the subject of the Wheatsheaf and all the ghostly goings on. I could sense his anger rising, burning through his reddened face. All this trauma had affected him as much as it had ripped me apart inside. Hearing Mark talking from his heart, I was relieved that he was able to offload a lot of his frustration. He had tried to bury his exasperations inside his soul and it was now pouring out of him. All I could do was watch as he cried, and expressed his true feelings. As he poured his heart out, I could feel our bond growing strong once again. I felt hope and a warmness towards Mark, both of which had been in short supply of late.

The moment came to a halt, my hope evaporated in an instant. I noticed wispy threads of a black shadow appearing out of the corner of my right eye. Vague stirrings of movement appeared in the corner of the kitchen moving towards the hall. 'Mark stop!' I said in a quivering soft voice.

His faced changed from emotional towards fearful in an instant. 'What's the matter?' he asked quietly. I had no answers. I didn't look at him, unable to tear my eyes away from scanning around the kitchen. Then I saw it again, a dark churning shadow which seemed to shift around the room.

'Mark, there's a shadow forming in the corner.' I prayed he would see it too. 'Can you see it?' My heart was beating in of my mouth.

After looking around the kitchen, he shook his head to say he couldn't, as terror spread across his face.

The shadow began to take the shape of a tall, stockily built man. The attributes which were appearing weren't lost on me, I knew with dreaded certainty who this was. Oppressive energy began swirling around like a hurricane. The kitchen was drained of light as the inky black shadow thickened and roiled within itself. Now spinning menacingly, it started approaching me. Mark pulled me towards him in an attempt to protect me. His body heat dissipated the chill which was enveloping me. The black storm came ever closer, only feet away.

'Mark, help me!' I was now retching, my stomach churning. The shadow, inky black, held itself a few feet away from me. The thought crossed my mind that maybe, just maybe, it wouldn't come any closer when a face spun itself forward from the cloud. I knew instantly who this ugliness belonged to. In an unearthly move of speed, his face rushed at mine and stopped, just as unnaturally, right in front of my face. I was frozen with fear.

'SurPPRIIiiiisssee' he shouted, his foul spittle speckling my face. The stench of his breath assaulted my nostrils. Before I could lift an arm to clear my face of his vile spit, he ripped me from Mark's hold. I will never forget the helpless look on Mark's face as he struggled to protect me from something he couldn't see. Joseph had me by the throat, raising me off my chair. I can still remember the feeling of my legs dangling, my feet searching for the floor. I could hear Mark screaming at the entity as he tried desperately to pull me down to safety.

'Leave her alone, you bastard!! What the fuck is happening?' Mark tried to pull me back towards him but Joseph's strength was immense, his grip unforgiving. I could feel the roughness of each finger as they tightened around my throat like vice grips. I was panicking, trying to pull myself away from him as his black eyes looked directly into mine.

'It's time little girl! I am anxiously awaiting your return!' He suddenly let me go from a height. I plummeted down to the floor. Within an instant Mark was crouching by my side.

'Suzanne!! What the hell is going on? Jesus Christ are you okay? Has that evil twat gone?'

Even if there had been easy answers for Mark, I couldn't answer, unable to speak. A strange sensation started in my chest and began moving up my throat. My entire body was wracked with a pins and needles sensation. A white mist escaped from my lips as I exhaled. The mist vanished and light and calmness returned to the kitchen. As I was too weak to move a muscle and shaking like a leaf, Mark helped me up from the cold kitchen floor and guided me into the living room. He propped me up on the end of the settee where I collapsed next to Francesca. We both sat in silence, both of us in shock. Several minutes passed as we tried to compose ourselves. A movement in the hallway pulled my gaze in its direction. Incredulously, I saw Jessica, standing there, unmoving. She stood head down, her blindfold visible. Slowly she looked up at me. Tears fell from beneath the blindfold. It was then that I noticed the horrendous marks on her neck. Dark fingerprint bruises wrapped around her tiny neck. I looked away, it was too much to bear and when I looked back she had vanished. I felt her devastation, but knew there was nothing I could do for her at that moment. I would get to the bottom of this another day, for now I felt it was more important to help my family.

I broke down and told Mark exactly what had happened the night before. After what we had both just experienced I felt he had the right to be informed. We went upstairs and inspected the damage. He was quiet, just shaking his head in disbelief as his eyes scanned the room. He pulled me close, and I knew in my heart that he now saw this situation differently. He now understood the struggles I had coped with over those long ten days. However, this was small comfort, for I would have to face Joseph again the next day. My body was penetrated with arrows of fear for what tomorrow would bring. *How the hell would I find the strength to walk back into the lion's cage?* I needed to have a strategy, a direction to head in, a plan. I closed my weary eyes and pleaded to my guides. *Please break evil's hold on me. Help me to conquer Joseph.* Quietly, I prayed to find the weakness within his madness.

False Calm

'Momma.' A little voice woke me. Opening my eyes, I was greeted with my little Alex leaning over me. I couldn't help but laugh. He was trying with all his might to scramble up on the settee so he could be near me. 'Momma.' His little face was all smiles as he let out a chuckle, more than pleased that he had finally woken me. I stroked his hair and embraced his love. He wore a grin from ear to ear. This moment was a breath of fresh air. Wishing this family time would last forever, I kissed his cheek. Suddenly he disappeared out of sight and fell on the floor with a thud. Letting out an almighty cry for his mother's assistance I rushed to his aid, bent down and picked him up, holding him in my arms.

As we cuddled on the settee watching a cartoon, I realized I was unable to concentrate, my mind jumping from one thing to the next. I felt agitated, it was nearly impossible to shake the oppressive weight on my shoulders. Any little movement or sound made me jump.

Haunted by Joseph's surprise appearance the previous evening I felt my nerves on a knife's edge. My mind scrolled over those tenty-four hours. I tried to explain away happenings which made no sense. The daunting events of that night put me in a cloud of terror. *How can I possibly face this evil again?* I was thinking irrational thoughts, picturing all the possibilities of what would lie in store for me when I entered the Wheatsheaf again. Even the calmness of holding my son close couldn't help me to switch off. My mind was like a reel of film going round and round, showing the same clip over and over, an instant replay of my own personal horror story.

'There is no escape for me.' My heart felt full of holes. As quickly as Alex's love filled it, Joseph shot daggers of doubt through it, the love draining away instantly. I felt so empty. Looking into Alex's blue eyes, I could see so much love there, but my fears seemed to somehow drain me of any comfort.

Clinging tightly to Alex as he made himself comfortable lying beside me, I began to pray. Pleading with my guides and the angels, I asked them to show me a light so I could follow. 'Oh please, I beg you angels, make this nightmare come to an end.'

'Morning!' I jumped as Mark popped his head round the living room door. 'Would you like some tea and toast?' he asked cheerfully with a smile.

'Yes please,' I tried to return a smile.

'I see Alex got what he wanted then,' he remarked as he glanced down at him lying beside me. I cuddled him in closer and kissed the top of his head. 'Well it has taken him over an hour to wake you up. Little mama's boy hey?' Alex gave his dad a cheeky smile.

'Are you okay?' I questioned Mark. He glanced at me with a worried look on his face, he looked completely worn out. 'Did you get any sleep at all last night?'

'A little. Going to make your toast, be back in two minutes.' He quickly headed for the kitchen. *Maybe it's not the right time to talk.* I decided I would leave the previous night's ordeal alone for the time being.

Noticing the time was already 10:30 a.m., my heart sunk. 'Oh no!' I shouted through to Mark. 'I didn't get a chance to see Francesca this morning!' *Oh God. What's happening to me*? I gasped as I recollected the image of my daughter standing at the top of the landing which sent shivers running across my body. I had dearly wanted to see Francesca that morning, to make sure she was alright and I longed to feel her embrace. My heart seemed to be cracking from the weight of the strain over those twelve days and I felt I was sinking into the depths of despair. I was in a world of my own when Mark returned to the living room and handed me a plate of hot, buttered toast.

'I will leave your tea on the mantelpiece to cool down a bit.' He took a seat on the chair opposite me. 'Oh…by the way, Sam rang this morning, she wants you to ring her as soon as possible.' He stretched himself out in the chair and yawned. His face was etched with worry and fatigue.

'Okay, I will ring her later on.' As I tried to make conversation with Mark, I felt he was distant with me. I wondered if he was as preoccupied with his thoughts as I was with mine. He sat seemingly dazed, staring into space. He wasn't his normal cheery self, and, given the situation, I wasn't surprised.

'Before I forget Suzanne,' I could see him wracking his brains. 'Francesca went to school just fine, but with all the commotion she forgot to remind us about the school play this morning. We have to be there.'

'Oh shit!' I could have done without that on this particular morning.

'Come on Suzanne,' He stood up and held out his hand to help me raise my aching body from the settee. I wasn't feeling right at all, and hoped the bug I had been fighting wasn't making another appearance. 'You have about an hour before the play starts.'

Mark grabbed some clothes for Alex, his little cord pants and fluffy jumper. As soon as he spotted his Dad coming for him, he scrambled out of the living room door. He was away like a flash. Mark an after him and picked him up. All I could do was laugh, seeing him struggling in his Dad's arms until his little face went red with frustration. He hated interrupted play time or cuddle time. His worst moment of the day was getting dressed.

I raced up the stairs to get dressed, which felt like a task in itself. By the time we were all ready to walk out of the door, I glanced at both of them standing in front of me. Smiling to myself, I thought, *know where your heart lies Suzanne. My family are more to me than life itself.* I would make the effort today for Francesca's sake.

When we arrived at the school, I could see the other parents all lining up at the main gate, waiting for the big blue doors to open. The exertion of rushing about and getting to the play had set pains off in my chest. I was now certain that my chest infection was back with a vengeance.

'Oh for God's sake Mark. Look at the queue.' He nodded in agreement. Crippling pains were rushing across my chest, each breath I took felt like daggers cutting through me. Finally, the doors opened and we followed the other parents. A daunting feeling that I was on the brink of a meltdown made me feel vulnerable. Mark looked at me with concern and then pulled a bottle of blackcurrant juice from the bottom of the buggy. Overly warm, and now running a temperature I hoped the soothing drink would stave off another bout of coughing.

Finally, in our seats, Mark began to rub my back. He leaned in close and whispered into my ear. 'You need to go back to the doctor as soon as you possibly can.' He looked genuinely concerned for my health. I was beginning to worry as well but struggled like hell to hold it all together.

As the curtains opened my heart fluttered with pride. Francesca was standing in the centre of the stage. She spotted us instantly amongst the crowd and gave me a huge smile. As she recited her lines and cracked some funny jokes, her performance shone as bright as a star. Managing to capture the audience, her performance was exceptional. I was so proud of my daughter and admired her strength. Not many children could have matched her achievement that day, given how much strain she was going through in her private life. Her sweet smile melted everyone's hearts. When the curtains closed, I felt a lump forming in my throat. It was a very emotional moment.

Mark asked if I was alright as I wiped away a couple of escapee tears. I nodded. He wrapped his arms around me. 'Come on Suzanne.' He gave me a kiss on the top of my head. He could sense I was crumbling inside. 'I need to get you home.'

As we stood up to join the queue to leave, I jumped when I felt a little hand grasp mine. I looked to see my daughter's beautiful face, like an angel looking back at me. I bent down to hold her in my arms, feeling her little embrace. 'I am so proud of you,' I whispered.

'Thanks Mum,' she whispered back as she reached up to kiss my cheek. Pulling away to join the rest of her class, she turned and blew me a kiss. With a wave she disappeared from my sight.

On the way home Mark mentioned we needed to go shopping. There wasn't much in the cupboards for tea that night.

'What?' I shouted as we walked towards the car. Could he not see I was struggling with pain? Mark was frustrating the hell out of me. I couldn't find the strength for a five-minute walk let alone traipsing around buying groceries.

'Well I will wait in the car,' refusing point blank to set one foot out of the vehicle. Mark hummed and hawed as he walked out of my sight towards the shop's electronic door. I turned the heating to full, unable to get warm. I knew it was only a matter of time before my cough became uncontrollable and I could hear a slight wheeze when I exhaled. That hour had become a total chore. By the time I got home I was struggling to keep my eyes open, in desperate need of rest. I tried once again to put on a brave face, but Mark wasn't fooled. He saw right through me.

'Why don't you lie down and try and get some sleep?' he suggested. 'You need all your strength to be on full alert tonight.' He gently stroked my head. It seemed odd to feel the compassion now coming from him, but I was damned glad of it. I needed to know someone cared. A tight knot hit the bottom of my stomach, reality creeped up on me. Time was running short. It was now 1:45. Mark was right, no matter what happened, I had to find the courage to face Joseph or he would make mincemeat out of me any chance he could get. 'I will be here for you when you wake up.' I agreed to settle on the sofa, and as I closed my eyes, I felt safe and warm.

Waking up with a fright, my heart was pounding in my chest. I was hysterical, my body trembled all over as I felt a cold breeze rushing down my legs. *Oh God no, please don't let anything harm me.* I quickly jumped from the settee and headed towards the kitchen, when Francesca came rushing in.

'Mum, you're awake!!' She looked full of excitement. Once again, I was struck with the resilience of a child and secretly wished it could be bottled. The change in her character was remarkable in such a short space of time.

'How are you feeling'? I asked as we sat back down on the settee.

'I feel fine. I am happy Mum.' We passed a bit of time away chatting about her performance. I was relieved that the play had gone so well, boosting her confidence for the better. 'Mum, can I have a new rug for my room?' She didn't hold back when she described the burn mark on the floor near the bottom of her bed. I took the opportunity to see what she recalled of those horrid events, briefly asking her about it. 'I don't remember anything.' She shrugged it off and told me Mark needed my help in the kitchen.

I opened the door to see Mark setting up a board game on the dining room table. I smiled to see my favourite game Cluedo was nearly all set up and ready to play. I definitely was not going to miss out on the chance to play and spend some calm time with my family. I rolled the dice and we began.

The game was a wonderful diversion; a couple of hours flew by. Once the kids were settled in bed, my nerves became wound tight. I realized it was nearing the time to face Joseph again. Apprehensively, I began pacing around the kitchen, trying to visualize whether or not I would walk back into the house in one piece come the morning. A voice came to mind. 'Don't show him any fear, this is your destiny, to save the little girl and all the other lost souls of the Wheatsheaf.'

Jessica now occupied my thoughts. *Why had she appeared to me again? In attacking me had he attacked her as well? Did she leave my body to save herself?* I thought back to seeing the tell-tale bruising on her neck, the tears and her sullen image. I knew I had to defeat this monster.

My mind seemed shattered into a million shards. I needed to concentrate on psyching myself up for an uncertain battle, with no idea what the future held for me. While Mark was busy upstairs, I took a few minutes to ask my guides for protection and to call upon the archangels for help.

A vision came to me. I could see myself facing a black shadow standing at the top of the lounge near Joseph's corner. As it swept across the floor towards me, I yelled out in a rage. My heart was palpitating vigorously. I then heard footsteps above me, walking across the landing and then clomping down the stairs. Mark popped his head in through the living room door. 'Are you OK?'. Letting out a huge sigh of relief, I realized the footsteps had belonged to him.

'No, not really,' I answered, shying away from his gaze. 'I am frightened to go back in the pub,' courageously admitting my feelings.

'Well then, don't go,' he responded firmly but not in an abrasive tone.

'You know I have no other choice now,' I stared at him. 'If I don't go, he will come for me with a vengeance, and when I say me…I mean anything that is important to me. I am not prepared to watch my family suffer the consequences of Joseph's wrath. I couldn't live with myself if something happened to my family. It's a price I'm unwilling to pay, I have to protect you and the kids. I need to face him tonight.

As I stood up and began to put my coat on, Mark wrapped his arms around me. 'I love you Suzanne.'

I was stopped in my tracks, astonished to hear the words which had been non-existent over the past couple of weeks. I quickly turned to face him. Our lips entwined as we stood within our own embrace. We held each other so tightly.

'I have to go Mark.' As we ended our farewell with a passionate kiss, I turned and headed to the door. It was time to face my nemesis.

Trepidation

Turning the radio up to help drown out my thoughts, I drove out of my estate, en route to the pub. Terrifying visions of Joseph kept dragging my mind back into reflection. The feeling of hatred shocked me and battered my soul. I had never known it as strong from anyone, let alone myself. Aching flu-like pains left me squirming in my seat, they had now paired up with a dull headache. Eventually I managed to switch off and was able to concentrate on the drive. It was only a matter of time before I parked my car next to the trees behind the all too familiar whitewashed wall outside the pub.

A knot tightened around my heart, as I stepped out into the cool night. Gathering my things, I slowly walked around the corner and headed to the top of the bar. I could sense tonight wasn't going to be like the other dreaded nights I'd experienced in the past. This particular night felt so very different from anything I had ever encountered. I felt like death warmed up, but that wasn't it either. Unable to put a finger on where the disquiet was seeping from, my soul knew the truth, the source of my anxiety would be revealed soon enough.

Glancing through the window, I could see Sam and Phil, standing at the top of the bar, deep in conversation. I acknowledged them with a warm smile and hello. I placed my belongings on the table opposite theirs and set my bag on the floor.

'Hi Suzanne,' Sam approached me with a welcoming hug. 'How are you?' she asked whilst pulling up a stool and gesturing me to come and join them. 'What would you like to drink?'

'Just water, thanks Sam,' I fished about in my coat pocket for my flu and cold tablets.

Phil had been watching me and asked if I was okay. Reassuring him that I was, I placed the tablets in my mouth and gulped them down with my water. Having barely swallowed them, I was wracked with a deep cough.

'Your cough is worsening again Suzanne, have you been to the doctors?'

Taking a seat, I reassured him once more that I would be seeking medical help as soon as I could.

'We worry about you,' Sam went on. 'We have all seen a huge strip taken out of you over the past few days, and I don't for one second believe it's over and done with yet.'

I sat in silence for a while with my head bowed down, contemplating on whether or not I should open up and let them know what had happened in my home twenty-four hours earlier. Something was holding me back.

Looking at Sam, I asked how many people would be attending the visual that night. 'There will only be eight, Suzanne.' *Oh thank God, the less people to protect the better. I need my energy to be spent on confronting him once and for all.*

Phil began to confide in us, sharing his daunting fear that something evil watched over him every second of the day. He said he now constantly felt he must be on guard. He doubted himself and every move he made, which was abnormal for him. He looked to me for the answers. 'Why do I have such a strong link to this Joseph?' He turned to glance at Sam and I.

'Maybe it's because you are the present day landlord of this pub?' I suggested. 'Maybe he sees you as a threat. Here we are in 2004, and this is your domain. Remember the day you held the lease in your hands for the first time? Joseph was furious. He also hates the simple fact that you run the place in your own way, the way you see fit.' As I glanced at Phil, I could see the determination written all over his face.

'Yeah,' he nodded in agreement. 'That makes perfect sense to me. Thanks Suzanne.'

Within seconds, the subject changed and we found ourselves trying to formulate a plan for the night ahead. Ideas began flying from the top of my head. I was more than curious to know what Joseph's intentions were. *What's his game?* I began wracking my brain, trying to formulate a strategy. I knew one thing for certain. Joseph would have his plan for me set in stone, and if that failed, he was very adaptable. I needed to match him and more.

It was after 11.30 before the rest of the team arrived. Time was ticking away. I decided it was imperative to discuss with them what may lay ahead. The team all settled and became subdued. As I went on, I looked into each one of their faces. It was plain to see, their facial expressions spoke volumes to me, they were petrified. Needing each and every one of them behind me one hundred percent, I had to reassure them and build them up.

Thinking quickly, I suggested we all make ourselves comfortable in the safe zone. I remembered that the best way to squelch fear was to find refuge. Everyone readily agreed, and began moving. I gathered my belongings and reached for my bag on the floor. It was then that a bolt of pain struck the back of my neck, the discomfort came so quickly and hard it made me jump.

Spinning around to face the top of the bar, I spotted a familiar black mist circulating around the door, directly in front of me. As I looked more intently at the mist, I could make out Joseph, his oppressive presence lingering in the shadows. My body went rigid with shock. I let out a gasp as I saw Joseph's face meld into the glass, like a warped image within an antique photo from the past. 'Oh God not again!' I shouted out. Sam and Phil walked quickly toward me asking me if I was alright. Sam held my arm to give comfort.

'Jesus, its freezing over here!' Sam exclaimed nervously. Her face showed the penny had dropped. A curtain of realization dropped across her face. 'We are not alone, are we Suzanne?'

'He is staring at me through the glass.' I whispered, pointing to his menacing face glaring in my direction. Phil and Sam both turned to where I had just pointed. Sam quietly told me she couldn't see anything, but Phil asked where the entity was… exactly.

'Right in the centre of the window, his head brushes the top of the casement.'

'Okay,' he said in a firm and determined tone. 'Joseph…we have had enough of you.' He stormed closer to the entity. My body began trembling as I shouted at Phil to move back. Phil held his ground, ignoring me.

'Phil!' Sam shouted sternly. 'Step away from the bloody door!! Do what Suzanne has asked!' He was standing only a few inches from the door.

'Listen… It's my bloody pub not his!' He then looked at me and pointed behind him. 'Tell this wanker to sling his hook!'

By this time, I was pleading and begging Phil to move away from the door. The dim light which had previously lit the corridor began to darken. The area directly behind him turned black. A grey mist began oozing around the door, seeping in at every gap and crevice. Horrid, sizzling noises began coming from the door. Phil turned towards the creaks and stepped quickly back to us. We now stood in amazement as a crackly frost started to spread across the glass like a cancer. I stood with my hand over my mouth to stifle my screams.

The bar was absolutely silent. The rest of the group quietly walked up behind the three of us to witness a figure transform in front of us. Crystals of frost formed Joseph's image, a frozen portrait to make any artist envious, every detail of his hatred painted in ice. He stared straight through me. The door began to vibrate and bang continuously, the metallic rattle of the hinges filled the corridor. 'Sam… take the rest of the team to the safe zone.' I turned to see the entire group right behind me, unwilling to move and leave me to my own devices. 'Go…don't worry, I will be okay.' The door was still slamming as I heard the team head to the safe zone.

Joseph's face was in a full scowl, filled with rage. I could see him backing away into the shadows. 'It's time little girl,' he growled as he let his energy slip from the room. The temperature very quickly returned to normal. I looked closely at the window in the door. The frost had vanished, no traces of moisture or one drop of condensation remained. I stood near the bar in complete silence for several minutes, unconvinced that he wouldn't jump out once more and tear me to shreds.

'Suzanne.' I heard Sam's voice.

Turning towards her, I noticed her now out of the safe zone and standing anxiously at the bar.

'Has he gone?' she whispered.

I nodded a yes in reply. It was now time to join the rest of the group.

'Come here for a minute Suzanne.' She placed a hand on my shoulder to command my attention. 'This ordeal is getting out of hand.' Her face showed deep concern for me. 'Come and join the rest of the team. Take a few minutes out. Because if we are shaken up by this, God only knows what you're going through at this moment.'

'Too be perfectly honest Sam, it has knocked the wind out of my sails. He certainly didn't waste any time to set the mood.' I half smiled at her as we walked back to the safe zone.

On returning to our refuge I noticed that most of the group were huddled up together. Their tension filled bodies pinned to their seats. They were almost sitting on each other's knees. 'Are you all okay?'

'Yes.' Chris spoke for all of them. Glancing across each person, it became quite obvious that they were grasping at anything to keep them safe. Each one searched my face for a sign of leadership and words to calm their fears.

'It's going to be alright.' I conjured up a reassuring smile from thin air. I advised the group to relax as much as possible given the situation. Joseph lapped up negative emotions like a kitten with its first saucer of cream. 'This is the safe area. He cannot touch us while we are protected.' They unstuck themselves from one another and leaned back more comfortably in their seats. Their anxiety slowly starting to ebb.

Noticing that I was fiddling with my rosary and clutching the cross for dear life, Phil and Denise asked me if I was alright. 'You must be a nervous wreck,' Phil added and then proceeded to compliment me on the manner in which I stood up to the scowling entity in the bar.

'Oh,' Denise stopped to let out a laugh, 'If that was me,' she pointed to her chest, 'I would have had to run a mile. I don't know which would be worse, facing that horrible bastard or the stench from my knickers.'

I burst out laughing uncontrollably as Denise set the scene in my mind. 'I would be back in my house and tucked up in bed by now. She pulled me closer and gave me a hug. 'I can't say it's going to be okay Suzanne, but by God go and give him a kick up the ass from all us, including the little girl.'

Now feeling emotional, I found it hard to take in everything that she had said. I was close to tears.

We all agreed not to let his threats get to us and decided we must stick together at all costs. We took some time to discuss the situation and by the end of our conversation, I was geared up and ready to go.

Confrontation

'Okay...we all know the drill,' to which the group all chimed out a YES in unison. 'Sam, can you recite the prayers once I step out into the lounge? Don't follow me though, I need to face him alone.'

'Are you sure about this?' she questioned.

'I'm sure Sam.' I picked up my candle and placed it in a small lantern, taking a deep breath. Feeling like an unarmed soldier heading off to battle, I stepped slowly into the lounge. Letting my eyes scan the room, seeking him out amidst the shadows, I began to pray. 'Please angels and guides protect me.'

Walking towards the stairs, I stopped to hear whispers from all around me. Men's hushed voices circulated around the room. Unable to pinpoint the direction or a source of the murmurings, my guard rose up. Walking a thin line between seeking him out and running to hide, I knew it wouldn't take much to tip the balance. Feeling like a fish out of water, I was up to my neck in despair. I took a minute to admonish myself, *stay focused, you're strong.*

After feeling only slightly more reassured, I took a deep breath and began to walk to the bottom of the stairs. I was convinced there was someone standing at the top landing.

'Suzanne,' I heard Sam whisper my name. I turned to see her head bobbing from the corner. 'We can see a shadow moving right behind you.'

'Where exactly, how far back?' I responded with panic quivering in my voice. My eyes darted around the room in desperation. *I need to be one step ahead of him at all times.* My mind reeled with a million and one things I needed to remember all at once.

'There,' she pointed, 'right above Joseph's corner!'

'Oh, fuck.' I ran my fingers through my hair. My head pounded, ready to burst at its seams. I was in two minds on whether or not to leave the group alone in the safe zone. 'Sam, keep everyone in the circle and continue reciting the prayers. Keep repeating them at all times.' I could hear a cry in her voice as she began calling out the Lord's Prayer.

Suddenly, I was positive I heard a man's cough coming from the top of the stairs. I looked up to see a reflection in the window, lit from the light above me. Apprehensively, I crept up the stairs, coming to a stop in the middle of the landing, where I found Paddy standing directly in front of me. His pointed and evil eyes matched the rage on his drawn face. He stood amongst two others, one on each side. Two men which I hadn't come across before.

'That's her,' he turned to one and then to the other. 'She has stirred up plenty of shit for us.' He now spoke down his nose at me.

Dumfounded I couldn't find any words to spray back at him, I was unable to speak.

He leaned slightly forward, to spit out his rage in my direction. As he snarled I saw his blackened, gritted teeth. 'He is coming for you,' he spat out. He then took a step towards me. And then another.

I stepped backwards down each step every time he came closer, never breaking my gaze from his. He came closer and closer and before I knew it I was standing just outside the safe zone. Turning to the group, I took a quick glance at them and asked if they were all okay.

'We are just a bit freaked out by shadow movements,' Sam answered coming within just inches of me. 'What happened to back you down the stairs?

'I've had a reunion with Paddy and a rather rude introduction to a couple of his pals at the top of the landing,' I answered, raising my eyebrow.

'Suzanne! Watch out!' She blurted while pointing to the bottom of the stairs. There, directly in front of me were the trio of shadows, one tellingly taller than the other two. They were steadily approaching me. Sam shouted to the others to come and see the ghosts which loomed threateningly, filling me with fear. As Paddy showed his true self, he ran towards me hissing. 'He will have your soul!!' he screamed.

Fight or flight took over. I was not about to be the target of his punches. I turned away from him, and threw a snarl over my shoulder. 'Let him fucking come then, because I am more than ready!!' I had obviously shocked him with my reaction because he stood motionless, sending evil stares in my direction to try and break me down. Realizing he could not, his energy faded as did that of his two partners. As they dissipated into the shadows, my heart continued racing. *What am I really up against?* I realized the depths to my question in silence. *Calm down.* I began focusing on taking deep breaths once more.

Glancing back to the group, who were hovering close to me, I read the story in their faces. They all had just witnessed something inexplicable. Denise stood clinging to Sam, one hand over her mouth. Phil asked if I was alright.

'Yeah... I think so. Keep an eye out for me everyone. I don't know where they will spring up next.' I was a bag of nerves standing alone in the middle of the lounge. *Please God help me...* I had no sooner sent out my plea when I heard a creaking sound to my right. I slowly turned towards the source. The cellar door had opened. 'Oh fuck!'

'What is it Suzanne? Phil murmured.

'The cellar door has just opened itself,' I said unable to tear my eyes away from the door. As I looked on in trepidation, it creaked open further. Under a veil of darkness, the silence seemed grim.

'Suzanne?' Phil whispered, 'Do you want me to accompany you?'

'No Phil, it's OK. Just keep alert at all times. Don't come out of the safe zone.' Now shaking, I stepped closer to the entrance to the cellar. Holding onto the door, I leaned forward and began searching for the light switch with my fingertips.

I screamed from the top of my lungs as Joseph's face lunged out of the darkness towards me. With one hand he grabbed my arm to pull me down into the cellar. I squealed for Phil as I flew downwards. The group were all calling out my name as I was whipped out of sight. I landed on my feet, gasping for air. My feet never touched one step. As my eyes adjusted to the dark, I could make out I was standing on the bottom step. The cellar door slammed shut.

'Suzanne!! Suzanne!' The group were banged and wiggled the door handle to the cellar. It would not budge. I was on the verge of a full blown panic attack.

'I'm okay,' I lied, trying to reassure them. My eyes were still trying to adjust to the pitch black, my heart pounding in chest. 'Oh my God,' I cried as a cold breeze raced down the back of my neck. I knew then he was standing directly behind me on the next step. Feeling icy chills crawling up my body from all directions, I knew I was surrounded. My right arm ached from being pulled down the first flight of stairs. My breathing felt out of control and my senses were numbed by the pitch darkness.

'Suzanne!' I could hear the group braying behind the door. Sam was crying and in hysterics, I had to call out to them.

'Sam don't worry!' I only managed to blurt out those three words before an icy cold grasp clasped my neck.

'I have you right where I want you,' he snarled. Where my senses had been numbed seconds ago, they were fully acute now. My eyes began to adjust, and my nose couldn't miss his putrid odour. I was without doubt confronted by Joseph. My mind raced, trying to figure out the best way to break away and escape his energy. I knew if I didn't, my world as I knew it would come to an end, I feared this was it.

'You can't escape me,' he growled, sending his rancid breath in my direction. His whole presence made me sick to the pit of my stomach. Standing motionless I waited for his next move. The team were screaming out my name and banging on the door in a panic.

'Suzanne?!' Phil shouted.

'I am going to kill you in time,' he whispered, his icy cold breath biting at my cheek. All I could do was pray to my guides, my defenceless body weakened by the strain of the confrontation. With a wood crunching bang, the cellar door flew open, slamming into the cellar wall. A torch beam cut through the darkness and shone into my face. My desperate prayers had been answered. Phil stampeded down the stairs in a panic. He wrapped his arms around me and guided me up the stairs. My legs felt dead.

'Please take me back to the safe zone.'

Phil tightened his hold on me, trying to comfort me. We were stopped in our tracks as the cellar door slammed shut. Joseph stood briefly, glaring, before his entity began to seep back into the lounge. He began following me, my head felt it would split as he began to break into my thoughts. I felt panicked as I felt my concentration blur. Phil gripped my right arm as he began to feel the evil presence filling the air surrounding us.

'Come on...' Phil tugged on my arm. I looked into his eyes and could sense his fear, which in turn triggered off an idea in my head. I slowly pulled my arm away from Phil and then turned to face him and the rest of the group. Straightening my back and standing perfectly still, I began to speak in a firm tone.

'No. He is destroying us piece by piece, trying to make me weak and feeding off our fear.'

'Come on Suzanne!' he demanded as he beckoned me towards the safe zone.

'I can't Phil, this is what he wants me to do.' I let out a sigh and asked my guides and angels to give me strength.

Phil remained, pleading with me to go within the circle.

'Go back to the safe zone. Go and protect the others Phil,' I pleaded as I stepped back from him. 'This is something I need to do.'

Sam and Denise were incredulous. 'No bloody way Suzanne!' Sam shouted. 'He is going to kill you.'

As Phil walked back to the group, my heart sank. 'I will be okay.' An intense pain began to hit the back of my throat. 'I've got to face him tonight.'

Walking into the centre of the lounge, I instantly realized the entity had moved. It was now pitch black near Joseph's corner. Deadly silence seemed to drag incessantly, making me anxious. All I could do was wait.

'Oh my God Suzanne!' Sam shouted, 'I've just seen him in the bar.'

'Where?'

Everyone's attention was drawn to her finger as she pointed to the area where you could see through the bar and beyond, towards the corridor.

I froze on the spot as everyone let out a yell.

'Suzanne! Come into the safe zone,' Chris shouted.

'No! If I don't stand up to him now I will never defeat him.' I was watching Sam's face as she relayed to me what his moves were.

She quickly turned and looked at me with a daunting look. 'Suzanne he has disappeared down the corridor, he is going to be behind you in seconds.' *Shit... what am I going to do?*

'Sam ask for help with the guidance prayer from my angel book.'

Threatening thuds and banging noises echoed down the corridor behind me. I turned around, but there was nothing but darkness. It was as if a blanket of gloom had veiled one part of the bar.

As I walked towards the obscured part of the bar, the team began shouting out warnings amidst their gasps. My life was in fate's hands. This would be my battle not his. As I stepped closer, I felt the temperature drop drastically. The hairs at the back of my neck stood up, which triggered a desire in me to take deep breaths. Focusing on holding it together, I took another step forward.

'Get out!' Joseph's voice made me jump back. I couldn't see him, but I knew he was only inches away from me.

'NO!' A surge of anger penetrated through my body as I stepped closer. I could feel him begin to press down on my shoulders. It was at that moment that a jolting pressure pushed me back, nearly knocking me off my feet. *What?! How can he push me so hard???* I had experienced physical attacks before at Joseph's ghostly hands, but there was a strength to him now which seemed exaggerated. As I was falling into a state of belated shock, and trying to hold my balance, another mighty push backwards nearly knocked me to the floor.

'I told you… GET OUUTTTT. Go and run little girl, time for you to realize that there is nowhere to hide!'

I was trying with all my might to keep my feet steady on the floor, but Joseph's strength continued to build. I tried to step back when I felt the force of his icy clutch around my neck. He lifted me in the air at a blurring speed and threw me through the air. I landed with full force on the pub floor, between a chair and a table, my legs and arms tangled around the furniture. There wasn't an inch of my body that wasn't aching or feeling bruised. My breathing was all to hell. I couldn't untangle my legs from the chair quick enough to get back up before he sped in and loomed above me. His filthy boots were now inches from my head. I raised my head to see him scowling down at me. His gaze made me feel like a bit of trash to be disposed of.

'Please leave me alone!!' I pleaded.

He bent down with unnatural speed, his movements now seemed awkward and jerky. Grabbing my throat, he pulled me up so I could smell the stench of his breath and leered at me, eye to eye. 'You're my next victim.' He blurted out between lips which formed a shit-eating grin. Hatred filled his voice, his eyes were black and fierce. 'Just you wait and see little girl.'

I was gasping for breath when the room began to shrink. Loud ringing filled my ears as the lights began to dim and my conscious self slipped away.

'Wake up Suzanne!'

I opened my eyes to find myself slumped in a chair.

Sam and Denise were sitting on the chairs next to me, one on each side. Sam was rubbing my hand, I could feel she was trembling inside. 'Let's get you a bit more comfortable.' She helped pull me up in the chair.

'How did I get here?'

Everyone in the group were silent, looking at me with sorrowful expressions on their faces. 'Chris picked you up off the floor. You had us worried sick, Suzanne. You were flat out for twenty minutes.' Sam's voice was filled with concern.

'Thank you.' I managed to give Chris a half smile. For several minutes I remained dazed in my chair. I couldn't understand how tonight had gone so wrong. From the moment I had entered the pub, Joseph was adamant that he would push me over the edge. Judging from my fainting performance a few minutes earlier, it was plain to see he was winning. It was all proof positive that he was trying to make good on each and every one of his threats.

All I had wanted to do was to stand up to him, but he had upped the ante. I was racking my brains when Phil gave me a nudge.

'He nearly killed you out there.'

I could feel him staring at me.

'He is going to take some force to get him out of this pub,' he said a bit too sternly.

'I know,' I agreed, not making eye contact. 'I'm not sure I can face him again.' He had shattered my thoughts and plans like a thin sheet of glass.

'Well Suzanne... you're in dangerous waters. This wasn't a battle it was a massacre!'

I rubbed my head to console my strain as Phil's words sunk in.

We all sat and discussed the night's events and tossed about ideas. I felt deflated and humiliated in front of the very people I had sworn to protect. I mentioned that I still felt several puzzle pieces were missing.

Sam spoke next. 'When I look back to when this all started, we were scared shitless then, it has gotten so much worse over the last few days. I wish we had left it alone now. It seems the minute we decided to communicate with the Ouija board, his strength multiplied. I truly believed we could find his weakness.'

The proverbial lightbulb flashed in my brain. 'Sam you are a genius,' I smiled with joy for the first time in days.

'Am I?' she chuckled. She looked completely flummoxed.

'You're bloody brilliant!!' I stood and began to pace back and forth in front of them. 'Right... we know we don't know a lot about this monster. We need to arm ourselves with as much information on him as we can. There are more questions than answers about him at the minute. I feel if we find out more about him we may find a weakness.' I came to a stop in front of the group. 'I think a trip to the library is in order. Maybe we can find a few more puzzle pieces within a history book or two. We need to find his Achilles' heel.'

By now, the whole group looked confused, but none more than Sam. I looked directly at her with a smile. 'Sam mentioned how Joseph's strength seemed to intensify when they experimented with the Ouija board. Maybe if we arm ourselves with more information we could maybe drain his energy the same way.'

'So a battle between you and Joseph on the Ouija board?' Sam questioned, not looking convinced.

'You have every right to be nervous about the board Sam, I fully understand where you're coming from. But if the board can build him up... maybe it can tear him down.' Secretly I hoped I could weaken him with the board, keeping him focused there rather than on breaking me into bits.

We all agreed it was worth a try. The group set a time to meet at the library. After a very grim night, optimism began to grow once more. As we walked towards the door, I quickly checked over my shoulder and caught a glimpse of his shadow. *I am coming for you this time Joseph... let the battle commence.*

A Miraculous Vision

I was becoming agonisingly aware that there was no way out of the mess I was now in. Uncertainty was lying like a boulder on my heart. *Who will win this conflict?* I was thinking too hard and knew I needed to try and get some sleep. As I rolled over and faced Mark, I found him fast asleep, mouth wide open trying to catch flies. I smiled to myself as I stroked his arm. He woke up, looked at me and smiled. 'Are you okay?' he asked as he laid his head on my shoulder.

'Yeah, I just can't sleep, my mind is going into overdrive.'

'What time is it?'

'Half past six,' I answered.

He stretched out trying to make himself comfortable. 'Come on, lay down here.' He patted the pillow. 'Try and get some sleep.'

I was too frightened to let myself relax. My mind was on alert; every sound was triggered alarm bells. I couldn't rest. Every time I closed my eyes, I could see him in the corridors of the pub, those evil eyes had corrupted my soul. I sat up. 'Mark... I've got to get up, I don't feel safe.' He leaned over to me

'What's the matter?' He pulled me back from my seated position to lay me back down. 'Come on, we will have a cuddle for five minutes.'

'Don't Mark, I can't rest.'

'Okay, okay.' He raised his hands away from me, sounding defeated. Jumping out of bed, he held out his hand. 'Come on. If you're restless let's go down stairs and I will put the fire on to keep you warm. Suzanne you look drained you need to unwind somehow.'

Laying on the settee and resting my head, I felt safer when Mark sat beside me. He lifted my legs and placed them on his lap. We sat in silence, both miles away with our thoughts. My head was pounding with strain. I willed myself to stop over-thinking and to shut down the horrible thoughts as I closed my eyes.

'Mom wake up!' I opened my eyes to find Francesca standing above me, her little face inches from mine. I jumped.

'Oh love, you gave me a fright.'

'Sorry Mum, but Dad asked me to wake you. Sam has been trying to get hold of you all day.'

'Right.' As I jumped up I could see her clutching my mobile in her hand.

'Suzanne?' I could hear Sam's voice long before I had the phone to my ear.

'Hello?' I rubbed my eyes, trying to move them from sleep mode.

'Oh thank God!' she exclaimed. She sounded terrified.

'What's the matter?' I questioned in a sleepy tone of voice.

'You're not going to believe this,' she said. ' Chris and I opened up this afternoon, the place was in a right mess!' Sam went on to explain that the chairs and tables were scattered all over the floor, the place was in a hell of a state.

'Oh no Sam, what in God's name are we going to do?' I said, more to ask myself than Sam.

'I don't know Suzanne,' she blurted. I could feel her frustration. She was crying and frightened. My heart sank to an all-time low. I felt responsible for the mess they had walked into that morning.

'I am so sorry Sam, I could have never even dreamt that he would vandalize the pub.'

'Oh no, Don't be sorry, we got a bloody shock of course, but there wasn't any damage. It was a huge setback to our systems. I am scared for you Suzanne. What will he do to you tonight? This has to come to a finale. We need to sort this before someone gets hurt.'

Her warning sent a shiver down my spine. I knew exactly who she was referring to, and I didn't feel confident or strong enough to face him.

'Oh by the way, Chris and I stopped at the library before work. We found some interesting photos of the Wheatsheaf in an old history book. You really need to see the picture of the pub back in the old days. It hasn't really changed one bit.'

Although I was surprised by the discovery of the photos, I was still distracted by the news of Joseph's little rampage. I tried to sound genuinely interested. 'Oh wow! It will be good to find out what the pub was like back in the 1900's.' I could hear the disinterest in my voice. As our conversation ended my soul felt bruised. I was feeling defeated. *Why can't he just leave me alone?* I wanted to yell from the top of my lungs. Joseph had made it perfectly clear he was capable of anything.

'Are you OK?' Mark asked as he joined me in the living room. I looked up to him. The kids were playing out of earshot in the dining room, so I took advantage of the moment.

'Sit down. I need to talk to you. I don't know what to do, Sam has just informed me that when she opened up today, the pub was trashed. There were tables and chairs scattered all over the place.'

'What? He trashed the pub? And you're thinking of going back there tonight?' He let out a sigh releasing his pent up fury. 'Seriously, think about this. You are playing with fire going back there. I am frightened for you.' He reached for my hand, holding it firmly. 'Don't go back please.'

I sighed and shook my head. 'Mark I have to do this... please understand.'

'I feel like we are running around in circles, this ordeal you're going through is tearing us apart. I love you.' Squeezing his hand tightly before I let it go, I reached over to hug him. We held each other, neither one wanting to let go.

'I feel so defenceless, I wish I could take all this pain away.'

We kissed to capture each other's love. Through life I had always been told that love would stand higher than any evil. I needed to believe that at that moment, more than at any other time in my life.

'I love you, I am always there for you Suzanne. Look it's 4 o'clock. Why don't you go and lay down for an hour.' He continued to cuddle me, trying to soothe me. 'Go and get some rest, you have a big night ahead.'

As I stood up to make my way towards the stairs, I realized that Mark was probably right. I needed the rest. It was time to try and put everything to the back of my mind. My body was exhausted from fighting my chest infection and the goings-on at the pub. As I laid on the bed and closed my eyes, I took deep breaths and focused on communicating with my guides. Through closed eyes I could see the room lighten. Distracted from my meditations, I quickly opened my eyes to see a bright light in the corner of the room. It glimmered and glowed. For the first time in a long while, I felt warmth inside my heart as the pure white light became brighter. I then heard a man's voice calling out my name.

'Suzanne, look into the light.'

I quickly shot up out of the bed to witness an angel appearing right in front of me. As he stepped closer, my body felt warm.

'We have heard your cry.'

In complete awe, all I could do was smile with wonderment as the figure stood in front of me. He was so inspiringly beautiful, with a golden light emanating from behind him. I could distinctly see a shield of armour and knew instantly that this was the Archangel Michael.

'Call my name out in your hour of need, I will be there to help you.'

With those words, the light faded and the vision had gone. My body was now feeling strong and radiant. This was a personal miracle, a calling from my angels to assist me. Wrapped in a warm blanket of relief and awe, I now felt I was ready to face whatever crossed my path.

'Mark!!' I shouted as I flew down the stairs. 'It's going to be okay!'

It had been a liberating experience. Filled with vibrancy and renewed confidence, I was geared up and ready to go.

'What's come over you?' He looked at me, confused. 'Are you OK?'

'Yes, I can honestly say I am fine,' I replied back with a smile.

I felt like a different person, completely in contrast to how desperate I had felt a mere hour earlier. For the first time in weeks, the strain had lifted from my shoulders. Finally, I could see a light at the end of a daunting black tunnel. I had a spring in my step that evening and my mind was clear. My family were able to see me smiling. Laughter flooded back into my home. I embraced quality family time watching a movie.

As the time drew closer to 8.30 p.m., I was focused and ready to face him. Reassuring myself that I was strong, I gave myself the proverbial Gill family pep talk. *Stand your ground and don't give up without a fight.* These were the words my Dad would have used in this situation. I was packing my bag when Francesca came into the kitchen.

'Mum?' she said. 'I've got something for you.'

'Oh thank you!'

She had handed me a CD. 'Listen to track number 6, it reminds me of the little girl you are helping in the pub.'

'Oh thank you little love.'

She gave me a huge hug and kissed me on the cheek. 'Come back home safe and sound Mum.'

I was struck by how much she had picked up about what was happening. I prayed that in time, this two-week period would become a blur to her. 'I will listen to the song, I promise. I also promise to come home safe and sound.'

'Good night Mum, I love you.'

'I love you too sweetheart, now you go to bed, I will be here to wake you up in the morning.'

It suddenly dawned on me that with any luck at the same time tomorrow, this battle could very well have been be drawn to a close. As the anticipation hit me, tears began racing down my cheeks. It would be the breakthrough I had cried out for. As I quickly composed myself, it was time to make a move.

'I am leaving now Mark.' Walking into the living room, I could see Alex was asleep in his arms. I leaned over and gave them both a kiss.

'I will wait up for you tonight.' He looked into my eyes. 'Be strong. See you in the morning.' He asked me to bend down towards him for another kiss. 'I love you Suzanne, now go and knock him into another dimension for me and the kids.'

I picked up my bags, opened the front door and stepped out into the night.

Confirmation

Whilst driving to the pub, I could feel the familiar knot in my stomach tightening. My previous confidence was beginning to ebb and adrenaline began to course through my body. I gave myself a very sharp talking-to. Needing this not to get the better of me, I decided to listen to the song which Fran had pointed out to me earlier. I clicked the CD to track six, and as I listened to the first line, "*Like a ghost don't need a key, your best friend I've come to be*," I couldn't contain the lump in my throat. The chorus followed with, "*If you're cold I'll keep you warm, if you're low just hold on, cause I will be your safety.*" In a flood of tears, I pulled into the next layby. Sitting on the edge of the road, I slowly pulled myself together. It was one of those moments in life, where it seemed a song had been written expressly for my particular situation. Astounded by the lyrics to the song, I was positive that it was a direct message to Jessica. I looked up to the stars in the sky and prayed for the angels and guides to assist me that night. I needed all the help I could scrape together to stand and fight him. Emotional meltdown over, I got back in the car and started up the engine. I was recharged and raring to go and face the unknown.

Turning into the car park, I noticed Chris walking towards the side of the pub. I flashed the headlights to catch his attention. Stepping out of the car, I could see him walking towards me. 'Hi Chris, how are you?'

As I walked towards him, I heard him answer with a sigh. 'I am OK.'

There was an uncomfortable pause as I waited for him to continue.

'Suzanne, I've been meaning to talk to you.' He reached out to hold my hand. I could see he wasn't his normal happy self. 'I am worried sick about you.' He looked into my eyes, he seemed completely lost. I could relate to every worry he had sitting on his shoulders. It must have taken a lot out of him witnessing what had happened the night before. I attempted to reassure him with a hug. 'I am going to be okay. Tonight will be okay. I need you and the team beside me.'

'I am with you all the way, you know that Suzanne.'

CONFIRMATION

As he pulled me closer, I was shocked by his reaction. This desperate showing of fear was completely out of character.

'I had a horrible dream about you.'

This admission triggered a sick feeling in the pit of my stomach.

'What was the dream about?'

As we walked towards the doors leading to the lounge, he painted a picture for me. 'It was horrible,' he sighed. 'You were trapped in the cellar and Joseph was hitting you. With an unbelievable force he thrashed you around the room like a rag doll.' His next statement made me want to run and hide. 'Oh God,' he faltered. 'You are wearing a grey jumper. Oh no.' He pulled me closer to him and whispered in my ear. 'You were wearing the same top in my dream.'

I jumped out of my skin. 'Did you see me die?' I felt the blood drain from my face.

'No,' he said. 'I woke with a fright before the dream ended.'

'Well I hope it doesn't come true. But hey… I appreciate you telling me,' I lied through my teeth. There are absolutely no words in the English vocabulary to describe how I now felt. Chris wouldn't want to scare me on purpose, but I wished he had kept it to himself. I had enough to contend with. 'Come on Chris,' I added, as I opened the door. 'Let's see what tonight brings.' I hoped to hell that justice would rule. There had to be an end tonight, once and for all.

The team had been anxiously waiting for me in the safe zone. Denise waved me over, and after the usual routine greetings she mentioned that they had something to show me.

'Oh great!' I said, trying to shake off the ominous feeling Chris had left me with. With a forced smile I sat down and joined them. I felt we had never been away from this pub and one day seemed to blur into the next. My world had become one hell of a rollercoaster ride with the Wheatsheaf taking up all the seats

'Look what I've got in my hand.' Denise was waving a book about in front of me.

'What have we here?' I asked as she handed the book over to me. The book was bound in bottle green leather. On the cover, there was a picture of two old miners, looking as time-worn as the book itself. I secretly hoped this history book was holding more puzzle pieces. It was titled simply, The Boldon Book, Past and Present. I wasted no time in opening it and flicking quickly through the pages. 'Thank you Denise.'

Scanning quickly through the book, I was stopped in my tracks, when

I came to a page titled Day Out to Tynemouth. There was an old photograph of a group of men standing outside the Wheatsheaf. Looking into every one of those faces from the past, my attention was immediately drawn to the image of a man who stood away from the crowd. Although the photo was a bit grainy and dog eared with the passage of time, there was no mistaking his distinguishing characteristics. He had silver hair and a well-groomed moustache. 'OH... MY... GOD... That's the man who threw Joseph out of the pub in my vision.' As I read through the script underneath the picture, it stated that George was the barman at the Wheatsheaf pub, Boldon. I kept my finger over his image, as I looked deep within the picture. Slowly, hesitating over each figure, I recognised another man standing next to the car in the photo. I pointed him out to Chris. 'There's the man who confronted me with Paddy at the top of the stairs a few nights ago.

'Oh yes... I remember being threatened in the middle of the corridor,' he said.

I was fully focused on the photo when a cold shiver rushed down my spine. At first glance, I dismissed the thought that the figure I was fixated on was Joseph. But as I looked more closely, I was convinced. It was without a doubt Joseph. He was mixed in with the other men in the group. Only his head and shoulders were visible in the photo, but it was enough. There was no mistaking the broadness of his upper chest and I had seen his evil glare often enough to know it was him.

Phil had been watching me and saw the change in my face as I studied the photograph. 'What have you found?' he asked. 'Let's have a look.'

'There he is.' I pointed him out to Chris and Phil and then handed them the book. Feeling relieved to find him in the picture, everyone would now be able to relate to how I had described him. Although I knew the group were behind me completely, it was nice to have the confirmation that I was on the right track. Chris looked at me and nodded.

'He was just what I imagined him to look like.'

As he passed it around, I sat back in amazement. Finally, we were getting somewhere. I now had the pictures to prove his horrid existence. Denise broke my train of thought.

'Suzanne, you've been very brave going through all this.' She gave me a faint smile and then looked back down at the book in her hand. 'Looking at him has sent a wave of fear to my heart. You need to know we are all here to help you through the battle ahead of you.'

'Thank you,' I replied. I then sat quietly reflecting and listening to their comments on the photograph. We all became subdued and chatted about the history of the pub. It was then that Sam decided it had become entirely too serious. 'Oh my God Suzanne, if he looks this menacing in the picture, I can't imagine what he looks like as a ghost!'

I looked at her and laughed. 'Believe me, he is ten thousand times worse as a ghost.' She set a smile to try and lighten the mood. All Sam's little one liners were amazing, they made us all laugh. Thank God she didn't take life too seriously. Her sense of humour had pulled us through many a grim moment. The light heartedness was replaced all too soon by the gravity of the situation. We all decided on the plan for the night ahead. Phil stood up and began to go through the closing routine.

Looking around to see there were more people staying behind, I became confused. *Had he forgotten there were still customers in the pub?* I realized they were staying. I quickly got up and approached Phil, asking why there were more people attending this visual.

'Oh, I hope you don't mind, I brought a couple of friends over to witness tonight's finale.' He smiled.

'Actually Phil, I do mind.' This adds an intense extra pressure on my shoulders.' I pointed over to the group which now totalled fifteen. 'How the hell can I fight against Joseph and protect all of them?' I was more than a little sharp but had to put my point across. There were far too many people.

'Well I didn't realize it was putting an extra strain on you. Okay... I will let my friends watch for a little while and agree to make them leave if it gets to be too much.'

I was furious. How the hell would Phil know when it got too much? Had he slept through the past two weeks? I wanted to scream.

Everything was all over the place that night, nothing felt right. Now he was attempting to turn the visual into a fucking three ring circus. I for one, was sick to death of Joseph's twisted parlour tricks, and here was Phil showing Joseph off like a small boy with a new toy. I would have to keep my eye on him, it was unlike Phil to throw more worry my way. Now I was certain that this was part of Joseph's plan. He was affecting Phil. Joseph was now conjuring up obstacles to throw in front of me.

'Okay, but I'm warning you now... one sniff of trouble and they are out the bloody door.' I had to be firm with Phil, as it might have been his pub, but by God it was definitely my battle. A battle I was fighting for him, his staff and clientele in his precious Wheatsheaf. He was an authority figure, a strong member of the group. It was just like Joseph to slide a wedge between us and weaken a link. My sharp tone seemed to reel him in. His face fell and he suddenly looked embarrassed.

'Okay,' he said as he raised his hands in a show of defeat. 'I know the procedure, I am sorry I invited them. I should of ran it past you first.' He shook his head in disbelief. 'I don't know what I was thinking of.' A confused look fell across his face.

'It's alright Phil, let's get ready for the night ahead.' I didn't tell him that I felt he had been under Joseph's manipulating thumb. There would be time for that later. Phil switched off all the lights and as the temperature began to fall, shivers ran down my spine. I knew he was watching my every move.

'Okay everyone. We all need to be prepared and aware of how serious things may get. Joseph is very clever. He liked everyone to see him as the village hero, a proper Mr. Congeniality. We have all seen him in action. We also have seen him for the bully he really was and remains to be to this day. We have seen his temper and witnessed his strength. We all know he will stop at nothing. I have to be careful how I approach the situation.' I looked at their faces as they absorbed the prospects of the daunting night ahead. I needed to be one step ahead of his game. 'As you all know, we discussed using a Ouija board last night. We hope to use it to our advantage. The board magnified his strength at the beginning of this ordeal. I hope to try and weaken him with it now.' I paused and searched their faces. 'I have a plan, but I know you're not going to like it…but…if this plan goes the way I pray it does, we can conquer Joseph once and for all.' I then dropped the bomb. 'Instead of me working on the board, I want you all to go on the Ouija board to communicate with him. This will free me up.'

Denise was glaring at me. 'Okay,' she said. 'What if this makes him ten times stronger, as it did in the beginning? We will have a right night on our hands?'

I was nodding my head in agreement. 'Yes it could go horribly wrong, but if we never try, we will never know.' I looked around the group, I felt for every last one of them. They didn't have to put themselves there that night after being through so much, but their dedication was strong. It was a blessing to see. I then scanned the faces of the new guests, some watched on as though they were at a sporting event, a couple more looked disinterested. They more than certainly were going to have different looks on their faces when Joseph reared his head in our direction.

'Where do you want me to set up the board Suzanne?' Phil asked.

I pointed to the table that was sitting just mere inches away from Joseph's corner. I could hear the gasps coming from the rest of the group.

'No way am I going over there.' Denise looked at me directly. 'Not after what he did to you last night. I couldn't sleep a wink thinking about you being hauled down the cellar.'

I ended up resorting to pleading with her. 'Oh come on Denise,' I sighed, 'please do this for the little girl.'

'I can't believe I would ever say this,' she paused briefly. 'Okay I will go, but I am not happy about it.' She stood up and with a brusque tone asked where we needed to be seated.

'Don't worry, I won't let him hurt anyone. My main goal is to put myself on the front line. If anyone is going to be hurt, it's going to be me. Right, I need six volunteers for the board. Two men either side of a space to be left at the head of the table. I will cleanse the area when we know the rest of the seating arrangements.'

Everyone was on pins and needles. I had never experienced anything like it. It took a few minutes and a couple of debates before they all came to a mutual understanding of who would sit where. As I closed my eyes and took in deep breaths, I began asking my guides to draw in close to my aura. I also asked them to show me love and light. Finally, I asked them to fill the pub with white light to protect everyone in the pub.

Suddenly, a blue light appeared in front of me. The same angel who appeared earlier had manifested once more. Remembering his words, *Call my name out three times*, I began to speak to him. 'St. Michael, Archangel, look down on me tonight. Thank you for giving me the strength to help defeat Joseph. The blue light once again faded away and I let out a relieved sigh. I felt better within myself, my head felt clearer with a renewed clarity of thought. I knew I was ready. 'Okay let's do this.' I smiled confidently at the group. 'Phil? Are we ready to set up the Ouija board?'

I watched Phil as he placed the lettered pieces of paper in a circular pattern on the table. Starting from the letter A, and going around the table clockwise until he placed down the last few letters X Y Z. Then pieces of paper, one saying "Yes" the other saying "No" were placed in the middle of the circle. The "Yes" was placed to the left and the "No" to the right of the circle. He placed a plastic cover over the letters to aid the glass in sliding freely back and forth between the letters as the spirit answered questions which we would ask. I was intrigued to see the board in action, as I had never played on a Ouija board. It would be interesting to see what information came through, hopefully some more missing puzzle pieces came as well.

'Phil? How often did you play on the board before all of this came to a head?' He looked up at me.

'Oh… I think we were on it for a month at least. What intrigued me to use the board was the day the ghost walked around in the bar knocking people off their chairs and spilling their drinks.'

'Oh yes, I think Chris mentioned that story to me when I first met you all. It feels like a lifetime ago.' We both looked at each other and smiled in agreement.

'Okay, I am ready Suzanne.'

Nodding my head in respect to Phil's wonderfully arranged Ouija board, I was now ready to take a stand. 'You will more than likely feel his energy as you're going to be sitting on top of each other.' Chris said he would sit at the end if Phil sat on the other side of the table. Chris and Denise were sitting so close together, you couldn't put a match stick between them. The looks on everyone's faces were completely telling, I could see everyone was terrified. Their anxiety had definitely kicked in.

I had hairs on the back of my neck standing to attention and my stomach was in nervous knots. 'You are all safe; I won't let anything happen to you, I promise.' I had no sooner made my promise when I spotted an unfamiliar man. He was of heavy build and a bit obnoxious as he jeered and made fun of the newest members of the group who had been invited in by Phil. I wondered why I hadn't noticed him before.

Watching him for a moment, I realized that the newbies were ignoring his taunts. Suddenly the fear of God washed over me. *Please guides protect me.* The strain was already becoming unbearable and we hadn't yet started.

I checked the time, it was now 12.50. 'Is everyone ready?'

I looked at the six people on the board, they all had their fingers pressed on the glass. No one spoke.

'Okay here goes nothing,' I commented under my breath.

Sam came to my side, standing to my right with a notepad in her hand. She was reading through the questions we had jotted down earlier when planning our strategy.

The pub was thick with silence as I scanned the room. I couldn't see him, he wasn't breathing down my neck like he had twenty-four hours earlier. Sensing an uncomfortable presence around us, I felt we were all standing on a knife's edge. The atmosphere felt electric. All eyes were on me as the group and extras sat motionless. I knew it was time.

'Okay Joseph... let's do this!' I shouted over the cloying silence in the room.

My eyes moved constantly, darting here and there trying to watch every part of the lounge. Terrified he would shoot out of the dark corridor and drag me to another dimension, my heart began to race. The thought of being dragged by an arm down the cellar steps had convinced me I had to be on guard. Last night he had caught me unprepared and vulnerable, but not this time. *I ain't taking any shit off him tonight.*

'We're head to head tonight Joseph!' I called out his name repeatedly. 'Joseph come on... I am waiting for you!'

'Pssst... Suzanne...' Phil's voice was barely a whisper. He was pointing to the glass which they were using as a planchette on the board. It was wobbling underneath their fingers. I could hear the group gasping out as the glass began shaking out of control. *Oh God* 'Please hold on everyone! Keep focused, this is it!'

I couldn't move from the spot I was standing on, my legs were wobbling as much as the glass on the table. The temperature was also dropping by the second. I could feel the bitter cold draft coming from behind my legs then raising to my back. I instantly felt an evil presence standing behind me, watching me.

'Paddy,' I said as I turned around to see a tall shadow appear out of the dark corridor.

Everyone in the room stopped and stared at me. Anticipation was written all over their faces. I noticed Chris was trembling and sitting on the edge of his seat, the colour had drained from his face. Looking at Phil, I could see he was almost trying to sit on Denise's lap. They had to have been frightened to sit amongst Joseph's energy, as the gap between Chris and Phil had widened. I hadn't wanted them to go through this torture, but I knew it was the only way I could confront this monster.

I gasped as the glass began to rotate around the board, increasing its speed. Everyone's fingers were resting on the top of the glass, they were barely managing to keep up with it. The glass sped up again and moved frantically to the letters which spelled out the name, Joseph.

I asked Sam to proceed asking questions, as she buried her head within her papers. I was being careful with what I was staying, calm, forming my sentences while trying not to let my voice quiver. Paddy's energy was moving in closer behind me, I knew he would be listening, both for what I was planning and also to detect any weaknesses which I may show. *Don't get distracted by him,* I thought to myself. *Concentrate on the board, don't take your eyes off the rest of the group.* I looked around to see them all huddled on top of each other. Denise, Chris and Phil had become a bundle of nerves and packed themselves tightly together. All six members at the Ouija board were looking exhausted.

Sam began to ask the questions. 'What is your full name?' The glass began to fly across the board as Denise was voicing out the letters which once more spelled the name Joseph.

'Ask him the next question,' I nodded to Sam.

'In what year did you die?' The glass took off, scratching along the hard plastic cover.

'1915,' Denise shouted over the screeching noise from the board to confirm the answer. *This can't be Joseph, he had never been this co-operative with me. By now he would be calling me all the bitches under the sun. Something isn't right.* I kept on saying the words in my head. As the presence stepped away from behind me, I quickly spun around to see his long shadow move off towards the dark corridor. He showed himself, it was definitely Paddy.

The tall lanky shape gave him away. His narrowed facial structure was more suited to the shape of a hatchet than a face of a human. His overly long and bushy sideburns made his face seem even narrower. The simple tailcoat he wore was dusty and threadbare. He was now glaring at me; his eyes were boring a hole into my soul. He then awkwardly stepped back further into the darkness. I seized this brief moment of opportunity to close my eyes for a second and question my guides. *How many evil energies am I up against?* A voice came to my mind in answer to my question. *Five dark spirits are waiting for Joseph's call to attack you Suzanne.* This wasn't making a shred of sense. It left me asking myself a few questions, but there was one which burned brighter than the others. *So, if the spirit on the board right now isn't Paddy or Joseph, who the hell are the group communicating with?* This thought led my mind in a completely new direction, and then the penny dropped. I broke Sam's next question

'Sam? Could you ask this spirit what its true name is?'

She looked through her notes and then glanced over to me looking confused as to why we had to repeat the same question, but complied with my request.

She raised her head to talk to the spirit on the board. 'What is your true name?' The glass squeaked across the board.

'Joseph,' Denise replied.

The glass wouldn't rest. It reeled out his name numerous times. 'Joseph…Joseph…Joseph.'

I was now convinced it wasn't him. I jumped when I saw two dark shapes appear above Chris and Phil's heads. They were two very dark spirits controlling the board. They were standing in for Joseph, doing a poor impersonation. I watched for a few seconds with amazement as the spirits had their eyes on me, but could spell out the questions in perfect order, simultaneously. I was feeling frustrated and angry as I shouted at them.

'What are your real names?'

The dark energies began to show their true forms. I could see they were both men, one slightly taller than the other. They were dressed in Victorian miner's clothing. Their clothes were worn and patched. Both had a bandana tied around their necks with a simple knot, and a flat black cap sitting loosely on their heads. When they noticed I could see their true form, they looked at each other in surprise. They then glared at me, sending shivers down my spine. Both the men threw hateful stares my way, trying to break me down. I looked away and stared at the floor. *Shit*, I said to myself as the reality of the situation kicked in. These two monkeys were on the board and Paddy was creeping about in the alleyway waiting to catch me out. I could feel two more energies in the top end of the bar. *Where the hell was Joseph*? I couldn't sense him in the room. I glanced at the group sitting at the board. They looked terrified, all their eyes were transfixed on me. They could see I wasn't myself. I must have looked like a right fool, dragging everyone onto the Ouija board only to be ambushed by a sinister task master. This evil bastard was playing us all like puppets on a string.

'Oh God.' *He is going to skin me alive tonight. I am lost. I don't know what to do or where to turn.* I knew that seconds were critical.

Suddenly a voice screamed in my head. *Get them off the board now!! It's a trap. He is coming for you now!*

'Get off the board everyone!! Oh my God.' I screamed, 'Get off the board, he is standing at the top of the stairs!!'

Everyone jumped as they drew their hands back off the glass. The group held each other, terrified and not knowing what to do next. The room was in absolute silence, but it was only the calm before the shit storm. We all began to hear footsteps coming along the corridor upstairs. The footfall was exaggerated. Thuds and bangs began to echo around the pub as the footsteps came closer. My heart was in my mouth. Looking up at the banister, I could see the light at the top begin to dim as his energy moved forward, peering down the stairs. Then there was a toxic deadly silence as we all waited for his next move.

Ouija

I need more time. I was holding my head in my hands, asking my guides and angels to stop him. *Please God please help me.* Flashbacks of Joseph hurling me around my dining room a few nights ago and of being dragged by my arm down into the cellar, made me fully aware of what he was capable of. I had felt his strength.

The sound of stomping footsteps continued from the top of the landing. 'Oh shit,'

I looked at the rest of the group. The newbies in attendance were now fully attentive. What a surprise. I could see they were terrified.

'Do you hear the footsteps Sam?'

She responded to my question by shaking her head up and down. Her hand was clapped over her mouth in effort to evade screaming the place to the ground.

The stomping steps continued, commanding my attention. My eyes were transfixed to the top of the stairs. I could feel him moving nearer and my heart began to beat faster. He had my heart in his hands and was squeezing tight. A pain rapidly coursed around my chest. It was the last straw of evidence I needed to prove we were in danger. If I was attacked I couldn't possibly protect fifteen people. There were far too many people there. They had to go right then before it was too late. *I need to clear this pub right now.*

I quickly pulled Phil aside and gave him the orders to clear out the extras. The only ones to stay would be those who had been through this from the start. Thankfully, there was no resistance from him or the newbies. Their faces made it clear that they were happy to leave. It was just amazing to see them scamper out the door. I doubt Phil had ever cleared the pub as quickly.

'Right,' I said in a firm tone. 'Are we ready?' I let out a sigh of relief as I looked at the original faces smiling back at me and felt the extra weight lift off my shoulders.

'Okay, let's call Joseph to the board. Come on, I am here waiting for you.'

Looking around the room, I could hear faint whispers coming from the group.

'Shhh,' I whispered, as I strained to hear the footsteps sneaking up behind me. I didn't feel the need to turn around, I could sense it was Paddy and the rest of Joseph's cronies waiting to pounce on his command.

'Joseph! Come on, I am waiting for you,' I bellowed from the top of my lungs. 'It's just me and you now.'

Glancing quickly to the board, I saw the glass begin to scrape ever so slowly in tiny increments across the plastic. It made a faint sound, but it was enough to grab my attention.

The group gasped as the glass began to move on its own accord. I looked at everyone's faces etched again in disbelief.

'Don't take your fingers off it.'

The atmosphere seemed to thicken, making me gasp for a full breath. The glass screeched louder as it began to pick up speed, racing from one letter to the next, spelling out a sentence. Sam relayed the message.

'Fuck off you bitch.'

'That's a nice comment,' I snarled back sarcastically.

As I leaned against the table, he appeared in front of my eyes. His venomous glare crushing my soul. He held this glare and paired it with a growl. His eyes were the darkest pits of black I had ever seen. I took a deep breath and walked back to my position. The glass kept frenetically whizzing around the board. Deep down I knew this would be the only way to drain his energy and defeat him once and for all. Sam spoke again, relaying another message.

'You bitch; you will be out of my way soon.'

This sounded more like the Joseph we all knew too well. I was furious with rage. His presence brought out an anger in myself which I had never felt before.

'Don't you dare threaten me you ugly bastard,' I threw back. We just stood for several seconds glaring at each other before I proceeded. 'What gives you the right to traipse around the pub scaring people out of their wits? Who do you think you are? King fucking Kong?' I smiled sarcastically at him. 'Well you don't scare me with your morbid attitude towards the living.'

I waited for a reaction from him, firing all my anger and hatred towards his face. He didn't flinch. He stood there with his hand on the glass, staring into my eyes. Finally, I could feel his fury rising, his face began to twist into a frown. His usual scowl was beginning to contort his face. *This is the breakthrough I need to feed off his anger and take away his energy.*

'Did you get a massive thrill out of controlling innocent woman and children? I know the lost souls up in the attic are there because of your cruelty and neglect. I decided to switch it up a notch. 'Oh yes, let's not forget about the time all the men threw you out of the pub and left you in the back alley after giving you a kicking and a beating too,' I snarled as the venomous words left my lips.

'Suzanne?' Sam brought my attention back to the table as she pointed to the board.

I looked down to see the glass was sitting on the board next to the word 'No'.

'Oh really… it's the truth isn't it? They beat the living shit out of you, a right proper hiding, then threw you in the yard like a bit of rubbish.'

The glass vibrated over the word 'No'.

'Everyone hated you Joseph and it's surprising your spirit is still allowed anywhere near this pub. Poor Joseph… must have been very difficult to go from being the town hero to the village idiot.'

He glared at me, his face contorted into a sinister grin lined with hate. He spat and snarled at me. 'I will fucking kill you.'

I glanced down at the group, they looked fully terrified. They held onto each other's arms.

'Try not to show any fear,' I whispered, giving them a reassuring smile. I returned my attention to the matter at hand, trying to find Joseph's weakness. His face was full of anger and hatred and I knew exactly where he would direct it to.

'Piss off you whore,' Sam read out.

I screamed at him with everything I had. 'You have manipulated people for years. You have interfered with women and children in the worst possible sense of the word. You let innocent woman and children starve in that freezing attic space. You let them DIE!! You evil prick! I hate you for everything you have done.'

Sam looked at me. 'Ask him if he has been to my house.'

He glowered at me, whilst spelling out Sam's children's names and their dates of birth. He then followed it up with her partner's name.

I looked back at her. She was standing next to the board shouting. 'Over my dead body will you harm my family!'.

Joseph replied with "as you wish."

Now overcome with nausea, Sam nearly vomited with the shock of information Joseph had come out with. 'Suzanne? I think this has been a piss poor idea. Have you maybe bitten off more than you can chew?' She was glaring at me.

I didn't answer her. 'Stop it!' I shouted to him as I placed my hand on the table. 'Leave her the hell alone. If you want to get to someone, pick me, I am here.'

He replied with "Piss off I am getting sick of you."

The group were almost jumping off their seats with frustration. Then the scratching noise of glass against plastic returned. Sam refused to read any more overcome with everything taking place. Denise read out my children's names and what he wanted to do to them whilst they slept.

'You dare lay one finger on them.' I was shaking. 'You noxious evil bastard!'

He stood there, motionless without any reaction. He knew he was hitting a few nerves between Sam and I. I could see what he was playing at, trying to antagonize us in hope we would turn against each other. This was a worrying development. He had earlier affected Phil, nearly causing ructions, now he was working on Sam.

'Sam? Don't take his words to heart, he is trying to bring confrontation towards us all so he can cause a rift between us. It's his way of breaking us down.'

I could feel this battle drawing to a close and ending badly. Suddenly, I thought of my home, memories flooding back of happier times. I refused to let this carry on invading my life in any way, shape or form. The close bond I had with my family was slipping through my fingers, if it meant getting my family back by fighting against this vicious beast, then so be it. I snapped out of my daydream and quickly drew my attention back to what was occurring around me. Noticing the group sitting on a knife's edge, I knew their expectations of finishing this confrontation were fading. None of us had expected to witness such foul language or to hear the threats against those we love, coming from Joseph. I decided to step up my game.

I yelled at him 'Did you get caught torturing the children?'

'No,' Denise replied.

I asked continuous questions over the next several minutes, but the replies I got back were hurls of abuse. 'I have had enough of you and your foul mouth' I am going to call down George to come and turf you out of the pub again just like he did all those years ago.'

He was foaming from the mouth with rage as he sped the glass around the board from letter to letter. 'Fuck off you dirty little whore... I will kill you.' Denise read out every vile word.

'Oh really? Thanks for the lovely compliments.' I was staring at his menacing eyes. 'Who is George you ask?' I didn't wait for his reply. 'This was his pub.' I cocked my eyebrow and smirked at him. 'Well come on then, I am standing right in front of you.'

He snarled at me in disgust.

'Joseph you're all bark and no bite, you're just full of shit.'

He reacted just the way I wanted him to, his hand was squeezing the glass so tightly, I was surprised that it didn't shatter under the pressure. He glared more intensely at me. I noticed a smirk appear over his face at the exact moment I felt a coldness latching onto my back. With a shudder, I realized I was becoming surrounded with bad energy. I didn't need to turn around; I could feel the freezing cold breeze on the back of my neck. Sensing there were three in total, I remembered the advice my Dad had given me many years earlier. *If you're ever caught in a situation where you feel you're in a hostile environment, never just stand there. Always aim for the ring leader and take them down with you. Don't leave yourself wide open where you can be caught off guard.* With this knowledge in my mind, I felt a surge of strength inside my soul, a wave of electricity took over my body. *Keep him on the board* came the comforting message from my guides. *Don't become distracted by other influences.* I jumped as Sam's clear steady voice shouted out.

'Why Jessica? Why an innocent little girl?' Sam demanded an answer.

'She got in my way,' Denise solemnly read from the board. Thinking back to my Dad's advice regarding distractions, I knew I needed to take back the communication from Sam with Joseph.

'Got in the way of what?' I interrupted Sam. I waited for an answer, watching his every move. 'You're going down Joseph, even if I have to drag you to the pits of hell myself.'

He was furious with my threats, not liking the fact I seemed to be in control. I continued firing every question I could think of at him.

'Fuck off,' Denise said with shock appearing on her face. She hadn't expected to swear at me at any time that night.

'Aww Joseph,' I said shaking my head. I began talking down to him with a sarcastic manner as if he was nothing to me. 'Is this all you have?' I leaned over the table. 'To terrify people on the Ouija board... you sick little man?' I could feel his ire rising, his face was contorted with wrath.

'We can't keep up with him Suzanne,' Phil shouted over the scratching of the glass. I looked in horror to see them all struggling trying to keep up. Their arms were no doubt aching from the repetitive movements over the board and sweat had begun beading out on all their faces.

'Please, it's not going to be long now. I promise. Please stay on the board.'

'Okay Suzanne, we will try.' Phil nodded his head and bent down to watch the glass fly from one end of the table to the other violently. The table was now wobbling with the force of Joseph's presence on the board. I knew the time had come to raise his anger and release it away from him.

Walking over to the table, I placed my hand in the bucket of salt that was used for spiritual cleansing. I began to spray the salt on the floor to protect everyone surrounding the board and on the board. Stepping back, I opened up my prayer book, making a sign of the cross with my left hand. Holding the leather book in my right hand, I began to send down my guides and angels.

'I ask for Saint Michael to release the evil from this pub.' I looked into his eyes and could feel my strength building up against him. It was the breakthrough I had been waiting weeks for. For the first time, I could feel his fear. He was losing the battle, and finally breaking down in front of me.

'Joseph this is it now. I am ready to end this for good'

I started to manipulate every sentence he came out with on the board, I found myself in tune with his energy and was reading his thoughts. It all came naturally to me as I glared at him. 'Ask him another question.'

I looked at Denise and the rest of the group. They were gobsmacked at what they were experiencing. I could see they were in pain as they willed the muscles in their arms to continue. It was taking a toll on the group. I had nothing to lose. Completely in control, I resumed eye contact. I could see flashes of fear in his eyes.

'Could you ask him another question to get him riled up? Ask him why he got kicked out of the pub.' I began to notice that the answers to every question Denise asked of him were now coming back to me telepathically.

Replying back, his answers shook him up. He was furious as he realized I was his weakness. A weapon to strike him down once and for all. Pleading with the group to hold on for a couple more minutes, I knew this was my breakthrough.

Reading through his entire life of secrets like a book, I could see everything and everyone he had controlled upstairs. They came to me like flashes of light. Rapid snapshots of Joseph's memories exhibited themselves in my mind. His past actions were laid before me, as fresh and as clear as if I had lived through the nightmare myself. I could see and hear it all, women's cries and the men's shouts echoing down a long corridor. The groans of the starving in the attic as they took their last breath. Beaten, bruised and dejected adolescent girls, still young at heart locked in rooms by themselves. The sight and sounds of children crying as they were ripped from their mother's arms as the demoralized women were led away. Men coming and going down a long corridor.

'OH. MY. GOD. you owned a brothel!'

He glared at me. I could see he was panicking.

'I know everything now Joseph, everything. The things you did to those people; the horrors inflicted on the women and the girls, and the children. Oh my God the children. You sick horrible monster.' I was screaming at him as my strength seemed to fire out of my soul.

I looked to see the movements of the glass were slowing and weakening on the Ouija board. Looking at the group, I could see the relief that washed over them as they felt the energy began to leave the lounge. The oppressive atmosphere changed in the room. Feeling the weight lift off of my shoulders, I could finally see a light at the end of the tunnel. It was time for me to ask for St. Michael's assistance. As his sweet voice whispered in my right ear, I took my prayer book from Sam and began to call out St Michael's name three times. Reciting the prayer out loud, I began to hear the faint sound of horses galloping. As I continued the prayer, the noise became louder. I closed my eyes and let out a sigh, asking St Michael to cut away all disaster and tragedy which had occurred within the pub and to fill the void left behind with his love and light. A blanket of calmness setted over the room. I smelt an aroma of incense and candles, the serene scent of a church. I looked over to see Joseph walking past me. He looked different, practically transparent, I could see through his energy to the wall behind him. No longer wanting to make eye contact with me, he walked until his apparition completely vanished.

I turned to see the group looking ashen and exhausted. 'It's over, you can come off the board.' I bent down. Trying to fight back the tears, a lump formed in my throat. I lowered my head down to my knees with relief. I was nearly hitting the floor with pure exhaustion. I was mentally drained and aches raced through my body. I had taken a battering that night. Words couldn't describe the true sense of peace that filled my heart. It was like taking a breath of pure mountain air. A sense of tranquility had entered The Wheatsheaf.

I wasn't the only one to feel the love in the room. Raising my body, I looked up towards Sam and the rest of the group.

'Well done Suzanne,' Sam said in the midst of the silence that filled the room.

Everything became a little bit brighter. The room was cleansed. I walked over to the group who had formed a huge circle. Through tears and hugs we rejoiced at our success in the defeat of Joseph. I smiled from ear to ear. I was ecstatic, not because of the battle, but because I had managed to pull bravery from somewhere deep within. I had enabled myself to stand in front of my own worst nightmare.

We decided to celebrate with a good old fashioned cup of tea. I enjoyed hearing the sound of laughter and the chatting about Joseph's lovely phrases and polite threats. Denise broke everyone's conversation to give me a compliment.

'I feared for you tonight Suzanne,' she said as she placed her cup on the table in front of her. 'You are braver than you make yourself out to be. Well done.' She smiled and added, 'You should be proud of having stood up against him the way you did. I am going to miss our strange nights in The Wheatsheaf.'

We all smiled with one another. I reassured everyone I would be in contact. We still had a lot to go over with the history of the pub and visits to the library. As I looked at all of them, my team, I realized just what a remarkable bunch they were. They stood beside me through this entire fiasco, not once questioning my faith or letting me down in any way. We had been through one hell of an experience which none of us would ever forget in a hurry. Time was slipping away and the sun was rising, its warm rays poured through the windows at the top of the bar. My stomach felt tight as I realized it was time to leave the pub. Standing up from my seat, I walked towards the safe zone to pick up my bag. I quickly turned around to see everyone relaxed and sitting in Joseph's corner. It was wonderful to see. It had been the first time that we had enjoyed laughing and joking in the seats which we had all feared the most. This was no longer his domain. He would never again overshadow that corner, creeping about and watching the comings and goings at the pub.

As the night came to a close, my emotions were running high. These people had become like a second family to me. I couldn't yet digest that I wasn't going to come back to The Wheatsheaf the next night or the night after that. We all promised to keep in touch.

Walking out into the morning sunshine, my earlier elation had already begun to fade. I was feeling more emotional than I should have, given what I had achieved. I tried to put this down to the letdown which sometimes accompanies the finality of finishing a project. However, I doubted this was the case. As I approached my car I felt the tiniest sliver of fear. *What if this isn't over?* I couldn't help but think, *I may have won this battle but had I won the war?*

Sudden Popularity

Several days had come and gone since I walked out of the Wheatsheaf for the final time. I had felt so elated about what I had achieved there. The elation had dwindled with each passing day. Struggling to come to terms with what actually happened to me, I couldn't escape the trauma of the horrid memories which repeated themselves in my mind. I was literally reliving the haunting of the pub over and over again.

To top everything off, I couldn't sleep more than a few minutes at a time. I couldn't shake off the chest infection I'd carried like a monkey on my back all through The Wheatsheaf ordeal. Laying down seemed to irritate the cough, and I was positive I had pulled muscles in my back during coughing fits. My body was in desperate need of rest. I had reached the brink of exhaustion days ago. I felt empty inside; a big part of me couldn't come to terms with many of the things which had taken place. I doubted my abilities and wondered if I really had rid the pub of Joseph's evil presence. This left me with an aching dread in my heart. I found myself still constantly watching over my shoulder.

I had by this time begun battling with my mind, trying to let the whole sordid mess go and put it all behind me. Feeling deflated and alone, I tried to confide in Mark. However, he refused to let me open up to him, becoming frustrated every time I brought the subject up. It was as though he felt that just discussing it would drag Joseph to our doorstep. So I had to pretend everything was wonderful when it clearly wasn't. I needed to talk to someone about my experiences and desperately wanted that someone to be him. Craving his understanding, loneliness had affixed itself to my nature. He only seemed happy at the thought of me being home a lot more. I felt resentful at the thought of just being there to lighten his workload, but thankfully the kids were comforted by the time we spent together and the games we played as a family. I tried desperately hard to bring my family back together, united as we always had been in the past. Unfortunately, I could see cracks beginning to show in our relationship. There were things I wouldn't tolerate from him most days; we were becoming distant. It was a sobering reminder of how my involvement with The Wheatsheaf affected everything. Our lack of communication normally revolved around the pub.

Life came to a standstill. Finally, desperate for someone to listen, I enquired about seeking some counselling, hoping to come to terms with what had happened. But, like Mark, I felt a fear sweep over me. If I opened up and spoke of my experiences, would this make me more vulnerable to Joseph's energy, I couldn't bear facing him again. My emotional health worsened. Reality had hit home like a bullet wound to the heart. I doubted my achievements and questioned my gift. The worst thing was feeling I had failed in some way. *Would Joseph return after everything we had done to defeat him? Had I paid enough attention to the little girls' remains? Had I failed her in some way?* I hadn't seen her in recent days and longed for even a quick glimpse of her. My defeating Joseph had set everyone free in the bar, but had taken me prisoner with its horrors. My mind raced back to it again and again until I couldn't think anymore. I longed to find some peace in my heart and understanding of the reasons behind it all. The more I thought about the events of The Wheatsheaf, the more I faced a brick wall. There was no way around this fiasco, it was paining me to face life. I felt accustomed to wearing my glass mask, I had no other choice than to get on with it.

I didn't lose contact with Sam and Chris. They were my escape. Through them, I was able to capture a little piece of The Wheatsheaf, always asking if the pub had calmed down after the final Ouija board session. Chris was the one who spent the most time in the pub alongside Sam. Working the shifts together, they had noticed that everything had become quiet since that night. Sam felt she was working in a different pub, the place had settled now and was a lot calmer. I was relieved to know that their workspace now had a peaceful atmosphere. My mind sank back to replaying the events once more. Lost within my toxic daydream, I jumped with shock when my mobile rang. 'Hello?' I said, as I gasped for air.

'Hi Suzanne, how are you hon?' I recognized the funny tone of voice.

'Hi Sam, I am fine thanks, how are you?' There was a momentary pause before she answered. Listening to the music coming from Sam's background. I felt my heart drop, and grew tense as I waited to hear what she had to say, thinking the worst. I half expected her to break down, saying Joseph had come back with a vengeance.

'I have some brilliant news for you,' she said. I'm sure she could hear the excitement in my voice as I asked what the news was about. 'Well…one of Phil's relatives heard about the spooky goings on in the pub. She works for the papers and she wondered if we would be interested in sharing the story with the press?'.

'Fantastic,' I said to Sam. 'When do they want the meeting?'

'Hang on Suzanne, she is keen to collect all the footage to back up the story.'

'Oh…I am a bit uncertain about just handing that over,' I said. This would need some thinking over.

'Well that's the thing, she was wondering if you could bring the footage along with you when we meet.'

'Oh, great… yeah okay, let me know when the meeting is and I will be there.'

'They want it for tomorrow morning so they can get it in the evening chronicle for Monday's press!'

'Okay, are we meeting up in the pub?' I asked.

'Yes, could you be there for nine.?'

As soon as I got off the phone with Sam, I was liberated with the news. I quickly called Denise to ask if she could make it to the meeting.

An hour passed, I raced around the house making sure everything I would need was ready for tomorrow's meeting, I was on edge all night, I couldn't rest, Mark could sense I wasn't myself.

'Are you okay?' he asked without waiting for my answer. 'Do you think you should try and get some sleep.' I glanced at the time, it was already 10 o'clock.

'Maybe you're right, I need the rest… big day tomorrow.'

I was so excited that the story would be told for all to hear. I hoped and prayed that this was what I needed to convince myself to let it go. A big part of me still feared Joseph. I never ever mentioned his name anymore to anyone.

The next morning was hectic as usual. Trying to get Francesca ready for school and Alex fed at the same time was a bit daunting. Mark had gone to the corner shop and left me to fend for myself with a screaming baby in one ear and Francesca asking me where things were in the other. I could feel a migraine pulsating in my brain as I answered her questions and tried to hush Alex at the same time. I was so glad to hear the key being turned in the door and to see Mark appearing in the doorway with a pint of milk and the newspaper.

'Thank God you're back,' I sighed. 'It's been a bit hectic since you walked out the door.'

My patience was wearing thin as I picked up my bags containing the remains from The Wheatsheaf wall and a few other pieces of evidence and hurried Francesca out of the door. I was eager to get back to the pub to see if there was anything else occurring. I felt I had let Jessica down by not finding her body. I longed to know if she was safe and contented. I strained to hold back the tears.

Pulling up outside the school, I gave Francesca a hug before she went up to the yard to see her friends. I checked my phone, it was only 8.45 a.m., enough time for me to grab something to eat on the way to the pub. Nervously anticipating the day ahead, I looked in the mirror to check my appearance before the meeting. I definitely wasn't a picture of health at that moment and that just brought me down even further. *Come on, you can do this.* After a quick bite and the short drive, I found myself in the car park of The Wheatsheaf. I hadn't thought I would be back there so soon.

I opened the doors and walked into the lounge. I was greeted by an atmosphere which was calm and serene instead of oppressive. It should have made me feel at ease in my surroundings, but it didn't. Despite knowing he was defeated, I was on edge. The paradox between the inviting atmosphere and my inability to settle within it was unnerving. I still felt on guard, waiting for him to make his next move. I saw Sam and Chris sitting in the safe zone, They waved me over. I could see they were extremely excited about today. Smiles were plastered on their faces as I approached them.

'Hi Suzanne,' Sam beamed, while Chris took a sip of his drink and smiled at me, beckoning me to sit down.

Just then, Phil and Denise came to join us. Everyone was looking well and rested. They were joyful and liberated that it was finally over and that we would be getting much deserved recognition for the traumatic times we had all been through. We chatted for a while, reminiscing about the whole experience finally being over and sharing funny stories about our lives. It was just like old times; it was as if I had never left. I could have sat there all day and listened to them chatting. It made me feel understood, knowing they had been with me through the whole thing. We could relate to each other in ways no one else could have. I could talk to them about it and they would understand.

We bantered on for about twenty minutes when three people walked through. The first was a man, tall and slim, with black hair and dark brown eyes. He gave off a very uneasy feeling as he strutted into the bar. An air of false confidence surrounded him, he was analyzing his surroundings, obviously not impressed. He leaned in, whispering his opinions to the man beside him. The shorter of the two looked to be in his mid-fifties and balding. He wore a flannel shirt tucked into his light cream trousers. He just nodded to the taller man and took down notes, gesturing to the woman on his right. She had blonde hair that framed her face and bright blue eyes. From afar, by observing her happy and bubbly demeanor, you could tell she loved her job . She was completely at ease behind her camera as she walked around the pub snapping pictures.

Phil walked over to them and introduced himself before leading them over to join us.

'This is Andrew, Robert and Ashleigh,' Phil said as he gestured to the tall man, Andrew. He didn't look impressed at all and made haste in throwing us his "you are wasting my time look." Robert and Ashleigh seemed somewhat interested, but a bit wary at the same time. They all greeted us and sat down in the booth beside Sam.

'So, what's the story?' Andrew asked as he grabbed his notepad and pen from his bag. Phil started relaying the events that had gone on before I arrived and during our visuals. I could see Ashleigh was becoming more interested, she was leaning over the table with a hand over her open mouth. Andrew and Robert however, remained stony faced as they listened, jotting down notes as Phil chatted away, each of us adding to the story as the conversation unfolded.

'Who is the medium?' Ashleigh asked, looking between myself and Sam after we had finished relaying our parts of the story.

'I am,' I said huskily, clearing my throat before attempting to speak again. 'Please forgive my voice, I'm still in the middle of shifting a cold,' I smiled.

'That's fine,' Andrew replied coldly. He was a very arrogant man who thought his station in life was much higher than it was; I had an instant dislike of him.

'Can we go to where you found the remains and take some pictures?' Ashleigh asked, to which Phil quickly agreed and led us all upstairs.

I could feel my heart quickening as I followed them up. It brought back memories of that very first night. I couldn't help but be on edge as I took one step after another, hearing the camera clicking in front of me and watching the rest of the group continue to the hallway a few feet ahead of me. I managed to catch up and calm my erratic heartbeat before they went into the ladies' toilets. I could hear Sam describing her experiences. When I approached the group, I got a cold hard stare off Andrew. He obviously thought I was a fraudster and wasn't impressed with our recollection of the events over the last month or so. I was still on a high, knowing that the press were interested and had come to see us. We walked around upstairs for a while and I posed for some pictures. We continued to the room with the fireplace and the cold hit me like a wall, making my chest ache as I took the freezing air into my lungs.

Everyone looked around, you could see the press were astounded by the gaping hole in the wall; they all looked at each other in surprise. I could see that they were beginning to believe our story. They all turned to us and tried to mask the look of astonishment on their faces. They began to ask questions about why we had dug into the wall. We all had our turn to be questioned.

'Sam was the first one to start,' Phil replied giving a sly wink towards her.

'Yeah, she went at it hell bent for leather with the sledge hammer,' Chris chirped in.

We all agreed and told them about what we found.

'Can we see the evidence?' Robert asked. It was the first time he had spoken since we had been introduced; I assumed he was the silent type and didn't talk very much.

'Yes of course, they are in my bag downstairs,' I replied eager to show them.

We all made our way back down the stairs and gathered around the tables we had occupied earlier. It was still quiet, as usual for this time of day, no one was in the lounge. I could hear a few voices from within the bar and the sounds of a football game on the telly. I walked over to the table and grabbed my bag, removing a small box containing Jessica's remains, and placed them all in a neat row on the table.

Ashleigh commenced with taking pictures, while Andrew and Robert looked at all of the pieces and examined them before writing notes. They then asked us if the items I had laid out were the originals that we had removed from the wall. We assured them that they were and hadn't been tampered with in any way.

They seemed to be leaning towards the idea of our story being real as we showed them the footage of the mist and the photos of the little girl. They were in awe, I could see their faces filling with realization. I finally knew that we were going to get the recognition we deserved. The day was quickly coming to a close as we all posed for the final photos as a group. I was feeling a heavy strain on my chest as I tried to breathe and I knew I needed to go home and rest. Being ill didn't suppress feeling jubilant however, I was overjoyed with being recognized by the press. As I was driving home, I felt like death warmed up, but I couldn't help but smile, I was so eager to know what they would say and I was itching to see the printed article.

November 2
Jessica's Warning

Time had passed me by quickly. I had become a recluse, alienating myself from the outside world. Fighting every day to be my happy old self seemed impossible. Caught up in a vicious circle of events, there was no escaping the trauma that I had buried deep within me.

Listening to other people's everyday worries and catastrophes sounded so dull and dismal to me.

I felt the personal trauma I had endured at The Wheatsheaf couldn't be compared with everyone else's menial worries. Where I'd had compassion for people and their everyday strife before, indifference now stood in its place. I had no other choice but to try my best and keep my head down to the matters at hand. Throwing myself into reality with a kick start, I had skipped out of neutral and forced myself straight into first gear. I was desperate to find peace of mind and to put my anxieties to rest. Every day felt as if I was drowning in a dark black abyss. I hated what I was becoming. Pessimism and depression had partnered up within me. There was no one in sight to help me or listen to my worries.

Mark didn't give me the time of day anymore. Every time I even tried to mention The Wheatsheaf, it would spark an argument which sent me on another downhill spiral. I so longed to be happy again. Realizing I needed to stand on my own two feet as no one seemed to care, left me emotionally drained. Interspersed with emotional turmoil, I began having unsettling visions. People whose faces I had never laid eyes on before flashed before me with no warning. It was as if my mind had its own photograph album of people from another era. The continuous haunting images of children and women screaming in my head at random times, disturbed me no end. Even something as mundane as watching a film with the kids was interrupted by the quick flashes of dark shadowy figures in the corner of my eye. I would look to find nothing there and would doubt myself even further. Anxiety was now a constant companion. *Would there be no escaping the events of The Wheatsheaf?* The whole ordeal had switched a light on inside the recesses of my psyche. Trauma was now taking me on a journey. Venturing into the deepest of holes, I was falling fast.

I sat and tried to enjoy a hot lemon drink while contemplating what fate had in store for me. Eyes closed and deep in reflection, I nearly missed the gentle waft of warmth around me.

On opening my eyes, I caught a glimmer of white light floating right in front of me. I could feel the presence of little Jessica. Her love encircled me. My heart began to burst open with emotion. I felt privileged and relieved that she had come to visit me. I had worried incessantly about her well-being. Closing my eyes once again, I could see her spirit form as she communicated through my thoughts.

I am safe, don't worry for me. She smiled. Her golden hair flowed across her pretty little face.

All too soon, the vision left me. Her energy faded and was now replaced by something more unnerving. Piercing flashes of different colours began swirling around the living room. Trying to break this link, I opened my eyes. What I saw next filled me with dread. I found myself standing in the lounge of The Wheatsheaf Pub. *Oh my God what is happening?* As I glanced around the room, I tried to understand what was unfolding in front of me. *This must be a premonition. This can't be real!* I was gasping with shock, my heart was beating hard and fast. Certain that I heard a child's voice calling out my name, I turned to where the sound had come from. A little glimmer of light caught my eye. I could see it sparkling near the seating area in the safe zone. *It's Jessica.* I felt drawn towards her energy. Unexpectedly hearing Sam's voice, I turned to see her coming down the stairs. With a bunch of keys in one hand and her phone in the other, I heard her speak to the person on the other end.

'Oh it's okay,' she said as she went through the pub locking up.

I wanted to wave to her to capture her attention, but instinctively I knew she wouldn't see me. It was then that I noticed Chris working at the top end of the bar. I stood in the safe zone and divided my attention between Jessica's energy and watching Sam and Chris locking up. Suddenly, I heard the unmistakable sound of breaking glass. Chris had dropped a pint glass to the floor. I looked from the shards of glass up to his face. His face showed no emotion and his body had gone rigid. His eyes were glazed. His whole demeanor was more attuned to that of a zombie in a horror movie. I was certain that something had taken over his body. In disbelief, I watched as he turned his head towards me. What I saw in his face froze me with terror.

'Noooooooooooo,' I screamed before realizing no one would hear my cries. He snarled at me. His eyes were projecting evil daggers towards me. His intense glare fixed on me for far too long. Finally breaking his optical assault, he then turned and slowly walked towards the door at the top of the bar. As he disappeared from my vision, I knew he would come out at the top part of the lounge. Sam would be soon walking right into his hands.

'Sam,' I squealed, as I began hammering loudly on the post beside me to try and attract her attention. It was to no avail, tears of frustration poured down my cheeks. Chris reached out from the darkness and grabbed her. I felt totally inept as I watched him push her forcefully down the cellar steps. In hysterics, I wanted the vision to end so I could ring and warn her. But the horror continued as I witnessed Sam's assault before it actually had been committed. Hearing her screams echoing around the lounge, I was mortified with Chris's behaviour. He then stood motionless, looking down into the darkness of the cellar. Once again, he slowly turned his head towards me. He had transformed fully into Joseph. His true form had completely taken over Chris's body. Seeing the caustic personality of Joseph in the body of a kind and gentle man was an moment I could have done without. He growled at me.

'You!' he yelled, as I stood there with my mouth hanging open in disbelief. 'I am coming back for you.'

Oh God, please remove me from this horror. My prayer went unanswered as he turned his body and started running towards me like his feet had the wings of a dragon. His face was contorted with hatred for me. He began growling in a temper. 'I am going to kill you this time.'

Break the vision Suzanne, break the damn vision! Inches away from grabbing me, the thought of being hurled down the cellar steps for the second time, played over in my mind on instant replay. I screamed as Joseph came within a hair's breadth of my face. I could feel his freezing cold breath, laced with the odour of death. He quickly grabbed my arm and began heading for the cellar. With all the strength I could muster, I pulled my arm away from him and found myself on the floor in my sitting room with my cup in my hand. The vision had ended none too soon. Shaking and crying, I came to a couple of grim realizations. Number one was knowing my life was in jeopardy and number two was that Joseph was back with an unholy vengeance.

Picking myself up from the floor, I sat down on the end of the settee. My heart was racing unnaturally and mentally I felt on the brink of a complete meltdown. I was terrified to think he had wormed his way back into the pub. The only bright spot was seeing Jessica. The poor little mite had sent me this vision. It was her way of sending me a much needed warning. It had worked. Alarm bells were ringing in my head. He had grown stronger than ever before. His venomous glare in my vision clearly showed that he was out for revenge, he was ready to destroy me once and for all. The bottom of my world was crumbling apart underneath my feet. A tightening pain hit my heart like a lightning bolt. I knew I didn't think have any strength left in me to fight Joseph again.

'What am I going to do?' I said out loud through my tears of desperation. I was screaming inside, panicking, over all of the possibilities Joseph could take as he exacted his revenge upon me. He had placed my life on the line again. *Please someone help me.* I began praying for a saviour to appear right in front of me. Praying for them to show me the way through the horrific ordeal I was about to face. No one came.

In true surreal fashion, I glanced at the clock, 6.50 a.m. I wiped away the tears from my face. This was the way of life for me at that time, living within a nightmare while trying to carry on with a normal life amidst my family. It was almost time to call Francesca down for school. I had no choice but to shake off whatever happened and be Suzanne the loving mum. If the kids knew I had been up all night, it would have upset them. I learned very quickly how to hold it all together when I was around the family. Now an expert on bottling things up, I hoped the cork would hold steadfast.

I walked to the hallway and looked up the stairs to call for Francesca. Just as I was about to open my mouth, a little blonde head popped over the banister.

'Morning Mum,' Francesca replied sleepily as she rubbed her eyes.

'Come on down love, I will make your breakfast.' I turned to walk into the kitchen and took a deep breath. I was feeling completely shook up. *Come on Suzanne, you can find a way through this. Switch it off and concentrate on your daughter.*

'Here you go Francesca.' I walked back into the living room and placed the tray on her lap.

She sat back and enjoyed her breakfast. Her morning routine was to try and watch a Disney cartoon in peace, before Alex woke up and disrupted her with his high pitched screams. Hearing noises upstairs, I realized that Mark must be awake. He soon came down and peered his head into the living room.

'What time did you get up?' I answered by looking at him with a concerned frown. 'Did you come to bed at all last night Suzanne?'

I shook my head and noticed his face had fallen in disappointment.

'I couldn't sleep Mark; I have a lot on my mind.'

He looked at me and shook his head. 'Why what's the matter with you? I hope you're not sitting up all night reminiscing about the fucking Wheatsheaf again.'

I felt a rage fire up inside. I longed to tell him of the horrendous vision I had endured minutes prior but thought better of it. From his reaction to me not going to bed I doubted he would want to hear about it. I looked at him with a face of thunder.

'No, it's not about The Wheatsheaf. I genuinely couldn't sleep alright?'

'Right I was only asking,' he moaned as he waved his hand up and down with a "calm down" motion.

'Well you have hit a nerve with what you've just said,' I blurted out to put my point across. 'It's not nice to feel victimized by you. I have had enough of you pointing the finger at me all the time.' I decided to avoid an argument by asking Francesca to go and get ready for school.

'I love you Mum,' she whispered in my ear.

'I love you too,' I smiled trying to reserve my anger for Mark. Needing to get away from the house, I offered to drive her to school. She became excited as she remembered she had a request for me.

'Mum can I have five pounds? There's a book that's for sale at the book fair. Can I buy it please?'

I looked over to her and could see how eager she seemed. My avid little reader had become the first in her class to finish a book in the matter of half a day. I wondered if she was going to try and break her own record. We parked up in the school parking lot.

'Okay love,' I said as I pulled out a fiver from my purse.

'Thank you Mum!' She blew me a kiss as she closed the car door and ran through the school gates. I wasted no time in finding my phone to call Chris and warn him. Turning down the volume of the car radio, I heard Chris answer nearly straight away. We chatted for a few minutes before I decided to guide the conversation in a more serious manner. Before I managed to switch the topic, Chris had a question for me.

'Has Sam rang you?'

'No, I haven't heard from her in a couple of days.'

'Well she said something to me about a picture flying off the wall in the lounge, not far from Joseph's corner.'

'Oh no.' I came to the grim realization that maybe the premonition was a warning to be given to Sam. 'I will give her a ring after our call. Chris, I need to say that I fear he is back in the pub.'

There was a long pause before he spoke again. 'What makes you think he has come back?'

'I was visited by Joseph last night, in a vision. He showed himself possessing your body. Soon after that, he managed to push Sam down the cellar steps.' I went into detail on what had happened. Chris sounded worried on the phone and I could also feel he was concerned for me. I expressed how I felt about standing up to Joseph again, fearing it could send me off the edge. A panic attack began to affect my voice. I felt like I was choking which triggered off a bout of coughing. I could hear Chris on the other end of the phone asking if I was okay. 'Yes,' I blurted out as the cough settled. 'I am alright, I don't know where that came from.' I laughed to try and lighten the situation and make a joke out of a random panic attack.

Strangely, as soon as I put the phone down from speaking to Chris, Sam rang me. I wondered if I'd sent her a thought message that we needed to speak. 'Hi love, how are you?'

'I am good. Always working, but apart from that it's all okay. Suzanne, I don't know how to tell you this, but we have been experiencing strange goings on in the pub again.'

I listened as she described how the picture bolted off the wall and landed a few feet away from where she was standing. 'Oh no. Sam... I have some bad news to tell you as well.'

'Right,' she said. 'Let's hear it.' A waver had appeared in her voice.

'Well...I am convinced Joseph is back to his full strength. I started to tell her about the vision I had seen that morning and how Joseph had possessed Chris's body.

'Oh God,' she said, as I mentioned she was the victim in my vision. 'I don't want to be pushed down the stairs, why did he pick me?' Sam was furious that he was trying to threaten us both.

I could feel her frustration flowing through from her end of the line. We chatted for a while before we decided to take the next step. I was going to have to return to the pub to face another night. I asked her to contact the rest of the group and ask them if they could possibly all get together and have another visual, needing all the help I could possibly get. We made arrangements to all meet up on the upcoming Saturday night. When the call ended I felt disheartened. How was I going to talk Mark around to letting me go back into The Wheatsheaf? I knew he would refuse point blank to let me set one foot back in there.

I drove out of the car park and made my way back home, my mind was racing away with itself. I was trying to think of ways to prepare for Saturday night. I only had three days in which to get myself ready. One part of me was scared to death, another was curious to see if the activity in the pub was as bad as it had been previously. I had avoided going back. Knowing that my renewed interest was more than likely an evil force trying to lure me in too deep, I began to feel vulnerable. I didn't like the idea of any added pressure on both my physical and mental health. I had endured enough over those weeks in The Wheatsheaf.

Checking the time, 17.22 p.m., I realized with a panic that I was running late for work. *How I am supposed to be in Whitley Bay for half past six.?* I had only fifteen minutes to get up the stairs and make myself look presentable. I told Mark I was running late for work. He reassured me, telling me not to worry about the kids, he would make sure they were settled. In a right fettle with myself, I raced around like a mad woman. After twenty minutes, I was ready to walk out of the door. With quick kisses and good byes for the kids I rushed out. Off I went running towards my car, praying in the back of my mind that the rush hour traffic would have died down. I hoped to get to Whitley Bay in 40 minutes. It was going to take a miracle. I spun out of the estate and down the road, trying to decide on the quickest route. Choosing the back roads to avoid the A1 traffic, my mind raced as I drove to my destination.

By the time I finally arrived at the house booking, it was almost 7 p.m. On entering the lady's house, I was apologetic on why I was so late. Thankfully the lady was lovely. I could hear everyone in the living room laughing and chatting away.

Sitting upstairs waiting for my first customer to walk through the door, my mind couldn't switch off. Glimpses of Joseph's intense glare flashed through. Every time I thought back, the memories would send shivers down my spine.

'Hello,' came the voice of a young girl.

'Hi. Come and take a seat.' I proceeded through her reading and all the following readings, one by one. My customers all seemed very happy with the information they received from their loved ones on the other side. As my working night came to a close. I packed up and headed down the stairs to say goodbye to my customers. I walked to the car. I was relieved that everything had gone well. Looking at the clock on the dashboard and seeing it was 10.10 p.m., I mentally calculated the time that I would arrive home. It was going to take at least 30 minutes to get there. Knowing I was eager to speak to Mark, I hoped he would still be up. I needed to discuss going back to The Wheatsheaf. I was debating on whether or not to tell him anything. I knew that as soon as I landed it on him, he would hit the roof. As I pulled into the car park, I could see in my rear view mirror that the kitchen light was on. *Okay Suzanne, let's get this over with.*

The house was lovely and warm. I rested my head, leaning my body back into the chair and let out a sigh. Mark came into the room and handed me a cup of tea.

'There you go.' He gave me a smile.

'Thank you,' I said, placing the hot cup on the table beside me.

'How was your night?' He reached for the remote and turned the volume down on the telly.

At least I wouldn't be competing with the program for his undivided attention. 'My night went really well apart from being 40 minutes late due to bad traffic.'

'Oh well, as long as you got there,' he said. The topic swiftly changed course. 'I am really sorry for the way I behaved earlier on this morning.' He sank his shoulders down, clearly disappointed with himself.

'You need to know Mark, that what I went through has been very difficult to try and get over.' I was trying to push my point across before edging him into the idea of me going back into The Wheatsheaf. We chatted for a while, talking about a number of things, the kids and how they were growing up so fast. He was in his element if we were all happy.

'I have enjoyed you being around the house more Suzanne.'

I smiled at him in agreement. It had been hard dropping back into reality with a bang, but on the other hand I had so enjoyed seeing the kids more. I broke the conversation by saying I had a problem.

'What is it ?,' he asked as he leaned over to me with a worried look on his face.

'Well this morning I was sitting in the living room on my own, when a flash of light came to me like in the visions I've had before. Well,' I said as I raised my head to look at him. I could see I had captured his interest. 'I was back in The Wheatsheaf, and to make a long story short, Joseph possessed Chris's body. He then proceeded to push Sam down the cellar steps.'

He rose up and stood by the mirror next to the fireplace.

'Wait Mark, before you shoot out the door like you normally do. Hear me out please for God's sake.'

He sat back down on the chair and placed his head in his hands.

'Well, I rang Chris this morning and told him about my premonition. Not long after speaking to Chris, Sam called me. She went on to say that there had been some strange things happening in the pub over the past few days.'

He cleared his throat.

I could see the hurt spread across his face as each word poured out of my mouth. 'Well,' I hesitated. 'Can I go back in for one night?' He looked at me in disbelief.

'Are you prepared to go back into the pub again?'

'I think so,' I quietly answered as I reached out for his hand. 'Mark I love you and the kids. I don't want anything to come between us to jeopardize that.' I tried to reassure him. He bit back at me.

'But you are letting something come in between us. Joseph is in between us!' He shook his head, unwilling to believe what he was hearing. 'Every time you mention his name, my blood boils and my temper flares. Suzanne he nearly killed you, and now you want to go into the lion's cage to fight him again?'

I jumped up and stared at him. 'I know the predicament I was in when I tried to clear The Wheatsheaf. I promise this is my last time fighting this monster.'

He made no reply. He stood up and grabbed me, holding on to me with his arms wrapped around my neck.

I looked at the pale expression on his face and my heart melted. 'I don't want us to fight over The Wheatsheaf, but you better believe I will come back in one piece.'

We both sat down on the settee and held each other. I could feel the lump in my throat forming as I struggled to hold back the tears.

'Okay,' he said, letting out a sigh. 'I know this is going to take a lot of courage on your part to stand up to him again. I do believe in you Suzanne, but it's so hard to see you go through all of this alone.' He kissed the top of my head. 'When do you go back?'

'Saturday. Thank you from the bottom of my heart.'

He then looked at me with a stern glare. 'Mark my words Suzanne, if I find out it's been horrific I will step in and stop you from going back in for your own safety.'

I agreed with his orders. I could understand this would be hard on him as well. He had already spent far too many hours stuck in the house worrying about me. I knew I wouldn't want to trade places.

Midnight arrived and I was exhausted from lack of sleep. Mark decided to finish watching a movie he had taped earlier on and said he'd come up soon after. I stumbled up the stairs and checked on the kids, making sure they were settled, and then headed off to my room. It was a relief to be facing a full night's sleep in my bed for a change. After finding a comfy position, I closed my eyes and drifted quickly off to sleep.

'Mum?' Woken by Francesca's soft but insistent whisper, I bolted up to see her more clearly. She was sitting at the end of my bed.

'What's the matter love?'

She wasted no time in racing up and snuggling in beside me. 'I heard a little girl crying at the top of the landing, she woke me up.'

'It's okay,' I said as I stroked her hair. 'Shssh,' I said. I listened to her breathing become slower, as she drifted back to sleep. I laid awake wondering why this crying had happened tonight, especially with the vision still fresh in my mind. I eventually drifted back to sleep until the alarm clock woke us both up.

'Oh God, here we go again.' On climbing out of bed, I could hear Alex murmuring in the next room.

'Okay sunshine?' I peered into his bedroom. He was lying in his cot lifting his legs up and banging them down into the mattress, the entire cot was shaking from side to side. I went over to him and picked him up and took him down the stairs. Alex had woken up in one hell of a mood. He screamed continuously until I had his breakfast ready. It took me over an hour to pacify him and calm his little temper down. Alex was a little character when he was in a good mood, but he wasn't showing that side of himself that morning.

Soon it was time to drop Francesca off at school. The morning sped along and I wondered if I would could complete everything I needed to do. When I got home I sat and tried to organize myself with a to-do list. One major priority was to visit the church. I had often gone in the past and, given recent events, I was pining to set foot back within its serenity. It had always offered my soul great peace. With facing the danger of going back to The Wheatsheaf, I was desperate to ask God to give me strength. I put a little star beside the word church on my list. Sitting at the table and planning my day, I was interrupted with a phone call. The little screen on my phone read Aunty Eileen. I quickly answered.

'Hi girl!'

'Hi Aunty, how are you?'

'I am fine love, you know… the usual,' she laughed. She did make me chuckle as she chattered away on the phone. 'I am really ringing up to see if you're alright Suzanne.'

'Oh thanks for being concerned, I am fine Aunty, busy working and looking after the kids. The usual.' We both laughed at the terminology, and the multitude of meanings for the word usual.

'I do have some news on The Wheatsheaf though.' I settled myself in to tell my Aunty about the vision I had early yesterday morning.

'Ohhh no. Is Joseph coming back to take revenge?' Her voice took a deep and serious tone. Trying to brush off the gravity of the situation, I laughed.

'Yeah, I think he is ready for another battle.' I could tell she was worried for me, as she lived so far away and found it difficult to be there for me.

My family are all based in Liverpool which makes it hard to keep in touch with each other on a regular basis. I tried and make an effort to keep in regular contact with my Aunty, letting her know via text how things were going at The Wheatsheaf. I hadn't been as diligent over the past few days. We chatted for over an hour when the conversation reached a turning point.

'Look Suzanne, I don't want you going in there on your own this time girl.' She was adamant that she would book a train ticket. 'I don't want to meddle in your affairs Suzanne,' she commented, 'But my heart can't take another night staring at my phone waiting for a text to fly up. I will be on pins.'

I felt she was absolutely right. It would be nice to have some family support.

'Would you mind if I came up north to see you and the kids? I will try and get the train up tomorrow.'

'That's fine Aunty!'

'Are you able to pick me up from the train station?' I reassured her we would be there to pick her up. I was quite excited to have her up to visit for a little while, we get on so well. After the call, I walked into the living room with a buzzing feeling of relief. Mark asked if I was okay.

'Yeah, I am great. We need to get the spare bed set up though.'

'Why?' he asked with a confused look on his face.

'My Aunty Eileen is coming up tomorrow for the weekend. I hope you don't mind, she has just invited herself. She wants to come to The Wheatsheaf with me.

'Oh... no, of course I don't mind,' he said as he smiled. 'It's a relief to know she will be with you when you go back in tomorrow night.' Mark's last statement had made me realize how quickly the days had raced past. *Oh. My. God. Where had the time gone?* It's countdown time; the hour would soon approach and I would have to walk back into the unknown.

Father McDade

I checked the time, it was almost 3 p.m. Rushing out the door I went to collect Francesca from school. Hoping to save time, I planned on being one of the parents who stand near the gates to avoid being tangled in the crowd. I was watching out for my little blonde baby rushing out of the doors. I didn't have to wait long.

'Francesca!!' I shouted and waved to capture her attention.

'Hi Mum!' she called back, breaking into a run towards me.

'Have you had a good day at school?'

'Oh yes,' she answered looking pleased with herself. She commented on her homework saying she was going to get a golden certificate.

'Oh wow, Francesca, that's wonderful!' I gave her a big hug. With everything we had been through, I was so grateful my children were growing up seemingly happy and healthy. Recent events hadn't left any lasting effects on Francesca and her schooling. She always had a passion for school and it showed with her stellar grades. I let her know we were stopping at the church on the way home.

I had felt an urge to visit the little old church at Chesterley Street for days. Time was now of the essence. I hoped that I would be lucky enough to catch the priest, as I longed to find strength. I felt deep down that he would be the only one who could help me now. I could feel myself growing tense during the drive to the church and Francesca picked up on it. She could sense something was wrong, repeatedly asking if I was alright. I did my best to reassure her. As I turned into the car park over the road from the church, I spotted a silver car on the drive. *Get in! I might be in luck, hopefully Father McDade might have time to talk.* Walking over the road towards the entrance, Francesca mentioned she had never been in this church before.

'Well there's a first time for everything love.'

As we opened the big wooden doors, Francesca peered her head around the corner.

'Mum, Father is fixing the flowers on the altar.' I looked in and noticed the church was empty except for him. I walked down the aisle towards him. He hadn't heard us come in.

'Hello Father.'

He turned around surprised, recognizing me straight away. 'Oh Suzanne... Hello! how are you?' He gave me a welcoming smile.

'Father,' I blurted out. Collapsing near the altar, I broke down in front of him. 'Father please, I need your help.'

He dropped the spray of flowers and came rushing towards me. Francesca looked mortified.

'Come on Suzanne, let's get you into the parish house. Here Francesca, will you run ahead and open the door, I will look after your Mum.'

'Thank you Father.'

He gave me a smile and cradled me in his arms. I couldn't help but cry. All the stress and fear had finally come to a head, there was no stopping the emotional storm. This overwhelming release, in the arms of the priest, was the first time in recent days in which I had felt safe. Safety had become a rarity of late, I'd forgotten what a luxury it had become to me. Slowly I felt more comfortable and began to relax.

He guided me towards the door and then under an arch which opened into a large Edwardian style room with high walls. It was amazing to see behind the scenes of the house. I didn't recall ever being in that part of the church grounds. He was so nice and kind to Francesca, putting her at ease.

'Well then,' he said. 'I will put the kettle on and we can have a chat.'

' I am so sorry for landing on you today Father.'

'Oh don't worry Suzanne, it's so nice to see you and the little one.' He then disappeared into the little kitchen at the other end of the house. I have always liked Father McDade. Over the years he had been a blessing, as he had always taken the time to listen to my problems. He had been part of the church all of his life. He was in his 70's. He was a strong personality for the community, and I admired him for his dedication. A few minutes later he came back, carrying a tray in his hands.

'Here we go now,' he said with a smile. He placed the tray on the table in front of me. He was wearing his usual shirt and collar with a grey jumper over the top. His silver hair always made him look older than he was.

'Thank you Father, you didn't need to bother.'

'Oh you're alright, I was meaning to have a rest when I'd finished up a couple of jobs in the church. Besides, it gives me an excuse to sit down.' As he sat he let out a laugh.

I asked how things were going with the church.

'Oh it's going well Suzanne, I have my weddings at the weekends to keep me going.'

I smiled as he poured out my cup and gave me the sugar bowl.

'Well then,' he said as he took a seat opposite me at the long wooden table. He looked at Francesca sitting on the seat next to me. He glanced at us both, and asked if Francesca wanted to go and see the rabbits in the garden. 'I don't mind if you want to go and stroke them. They are in a pen along the side of the house.

I knew he had wanted to distract her, giving us a chance to talk. As he disappeared with Francesca, I could hear them both talking. I was more than grateful he was taking the time to listen to what was happening around me. When he came back in, I was cradling the warm cup in my hand and sipping the tea to calm my nerves.

'There we go,' he said as he walked in and sat down.

'Thank you.' I gave him a smile. He reached out his hand placing it on my shoulder.

'No problem Suzanne, don't worry. I'm not sure who you frightened worse, me or your little one when you broke down in the church.' He picked up his cup.

I began telling Father McDade everything from the beginning. As I was talking, I could see he was interested to know how I had got myself tangled in this horrific nightmare. I finished by explaining about Joseph and how I planned to go back in and fight him again tomorrow night.

'Well,' he said as he cleared his throat, 'what can I do to help you Suzanne?'

I couldn't get over how calm he was. It was as if he dealt with this type of thing every day, completely taking what I had told him in his stride. He grabbed my hand and asked if there was anything in particular I needed. I looked into his eyes and asked for peace.

He sat back and let out a sigh. 'This is off the cuff, and you didn't get this information from me.' He then stood and motioned for me to accompany him. We walked down the hall to a room on our right. It was like a theological treasure trove of testament books and bibles. I was confused; I had thought he was going to give me verbal information, but he began searching through the books. 'I've got something for you Suzanne.'

'I don't need anything Father.'

'Oh yes you do my child,' he said, as he continued searching through the titles along the spines of the antiquated books. 'Right I have a few suggestions.' He pulled out a couple of books from a shelf that was next to his old wooden desk. 'Now, where did I put that prayer book?' He bent down to search through the stacks of books standing in the corner. Moving his finger over the titles he came to a small leather bound volume. 'Ah here it is.' He opened it and began rifling through the timeworn pages. He began talking quietly to himself as he recited the verse and psalms numbers that he was searching for. 'There we are,' he said, as he sat down at his desk and began to mark some of the pages.

He looked up at me with a serious expression on his face. 'Before you think of reading out any of these words to this demon spirit, there are rules you must abide by. Number one, never say "I call you out". Number two, never say "I condemn you". It's always "God calls you out" and "God condemns you". Remember that well, or the prayer will be reversed and the demon could be sitting on your little shoulders, that's the last thing you need.'

'Okay Father.' I absorbed his advice.

'Now then, I have some special holy water that's been blessed by the Pope. I will decant some for you to take with you. Rule number three, only use it on yourself and the demon.' He handed me the book which I took from him with trembling hands.

The word 'demon' had now come up. Its serious connotations were sinking in. I felt this meeting would be one of the most important decisions I had made. Holding the book, I realized that coming to church was a key factor in preparing me to conquer Joseph the following night. I felt blessed holding the little book and grateful for Father's help. Deep in thought, I jumped when he spoke again.

'Right, I had this given to me a long time ago. I want you to have it.' He handed me an unusual silver cross, about the size of the palm of my hand.

I looked at its beautiful uniqueness. My fingers traced over its details, Jesus on the cross and God above him with his arms open wide. I then noticed an intricate symbol of a dove inside a triangle. I was shocked to think he wanted me to have this exquisite cross. 'You take it with you Suzanne, it will keep you safe.'

'Oh thank you Father, for all your help and kindness.'

We talked for a little while, knowing I would soon have to leave the security and peace of the church house. On saying our goodbyes, he gave me a hug and a smile.

'Don't worry, He is watching over you. Call for your Creator and He will be standing beside you.'

'Oh thank you Father, I am indebted to you. Thank you for the advice and sharing your knowledge.' I held the book and the cross protectively to my chest.

'It's fine Suzanne, I am always here if you need to come back and see me again.'

As I left the safety of the church house and walked around to collect Francesca, I felt lighter and more uplifted. It was as though a black cloud had lifted from my heart. As I felt strong for the first time in weeks, there was a lightness to my step as we walked back to the car.

On the journey home, Francesca busied herself with reading out the prayers and proverbs out loud. Every word she said, lifted my spirits even further. I was ready to face him now.

'Mum why did you cry in front of the priest?'

I stole a quick glance at her and reached for her little hand.

'It's nothing love, don't worry.'

She looked at me suspiciously as we pulled into the parking bay opposite our home.

'Francesca don't tell your Dad I broke down in front of the priest, he will only worry.'

Walking to the house, she turned and gave me a smile. 'Mum can I keep a hold of the cross for you until you need it.?

'Okay, you can borrow the cross, but I need it back for tomorrow night.'

As I walked into the house, I could see Alex was all ready for bed. He looked a picture in his Sponge Bob pyjamas. I walked into the living room. As soon as he clapped eyes on me, he yelled from the top of his lungs. He began holding out his little hands, wanting me to pick him up out of his Dad's arms.

'Hey little soldier.' I sat on the settee and gave him a cuddle.

'Did everything go well at the church?'

I was busy multi-tasking, holding on to Alex as he was wiggling around on my knee and taking off my coat at the same time.

'Yeah, I met up with Father McDade, he gave me a prayer book and a beautiful silver cross to protect me.'

'Oh wow!' Mark's response was overwhelming.

I had expected him to crack some snide remark about The Wheatsheaf, but he seemed genuinely happy for me. Winding down for the night, I read through the pages the priest had carefully marked for me. Fully occupied by the little blue prayer book, I lost track of time. Remembering I had an early start in the morning, I went through the mental list of things I would have to attend to the next day. I needed to be at the train station for 10.30 a.m. to pick up my Aunty, then plan for The Wheatsheaf the next night.

I suggested to Mark that I was going to have an early night. My mind was slowing down and I was beginning to yawn It was time to say goodbye to today and to try and wake up fresh the next morning. I was feeling prepared and went to bed with peace in my heart. Feeling grateful for being drawn to the church, I was convinced that I wouldn't have had the strength to face him otherwise. Without all the help from the priest, I was sure the ending to the next night might have gone horribly wrong. I was feeling grateful and content, for the first time in days. I laid my head on the pillow and drifted off to sleep.

Family Support

I woke up late that morning, Mark had decided to let me sleep in. He came into the room to wake me.

'Morning,' he said, as he stood over me at the end of our bed.

' What time is it Mark?'

'It's half past nine.'

'Oh God no.'

We were supposed to be at the train station for 10.30 to pick up Aunty Eileen. I jumped out of bed, my head in a whirlwind as I rushed around to get ready to leave. By the time I got up, quickly got dressed and rushed out of the door, I was feeling hassled. Mark had said he would come along for the ride and helped by getting Alex securely fastened into his car seat. I belted up and checked the time on the dashboard, 10.09.

'Shit Mark, we are going to be late.' I was halfway out of the estate as he clicked his seatbelt buckle into place. 'Give Aunty a call, and tell her we are stuck in traffic.'

He rattled around my handbag looking for my phone, and then rang the number on the top of my contact list. Driving towards Gateshead, I began scanning my mental maps, trying to remember the quickest route in my mind. Planning our drive to get to Newcastle Bridge before 10.30 a.m., I decided on the dual carriageway and sped towards our destination.

'Hi,' came Mark's voice.

'Hiya lad. How are you?'

Faintly hearing her voice on the other end of the phone, I asked him to put us on speakerphone. I jumped into the conversation.

'Hi Aunty, are you at the train station?'

'No. I am in Durham. There's been a delay at York, so I am going to be about thirty minutes late.'

Oh thank God. I slowed down the car and lowered my shoulders to let them relax.

With a broad Liverpudlian accent she asked, 'Why, are you at the train station now?'

'No we are stuck in traffic on the Tyne bridge, we should be there in about fifteen minutes. Don't worry about being late Aunty, we will grab a cuppa and meet you at the main entrance.'

'Oh I can't wait to see you all!'

I could hear the excitement over the phone. As we said goodbye, I could hear the relief in the tone of my voice. The one thing I do hate, is being late, especially when it comes to meeting and picking up my family. They aren't aware of the city centre area. I would never forgive myself if anything happened to her.

We finally made it to the entrance. Alex was squirming around, fighting against being buckled into his buggy; he hated to feel confined. Both Mark and I had our eyes glued to the station. We both scanned everyone departing from the trains. I walked towards the information desk.

'Suzanne!' I instantly recognized the accent and the familiar voice of my Aunty. Spinning around, I could see her making her way down the platform bridge. I ran towards her, the tears were streaming down my face, unable to contain my emotion. I wrapped my arms around her and gave her a huge hug.

'Hi babe,' she said as we stood and embraced each other. She gave me a long hard look and I knew instantly that she was picking up on the fact that I was feeling lost. She took my hand firmly. 'It's going to be okay Suzanne.' She gave me a big smile. 'Now... where is my little lad?'

I grabbed her bag from her hand and linked my arm with hers as we walked back to Mark and Alex. I waved them over to come and welcome Aunty Eileen to the northeast.

'Hi Eileen,' Mark said as he gave her a hug. 'You're well out of your depth coming up to Geordie town,' he commented as he laughed.

'You're right there,' she smiled back, playing along with his sense of humour. 'I'm starving,' she exclaimed. Thinking we all could all do with a nice breakfast, we walked back over the road from the train station and went into the Pink Lane cafe. I was well overdue a good wholesome meal to kickstart the day off. It was the first time I had sat and taken the time to eat something proper in days.

Aunty couldn't get over the size of Alex. 'My God Suzanne, he is the image of his dad.' I looked at her and laughed. If she only knew the half of it, between them both, they had become a spitting double act. I could also see the resemblance between my Aunty and I. We have very similar behaviour and sense of humour.

We had a lovely visit to the café. It was nice to have some quality time to reminisce about the good old days. But like all the good times during The Wheatsheaf turmoil, it quickly came to an end. I knew I needed to head home and settle down for the day, to prepare for the night ahead.

As we walked into the house, I was feeling relieved that I had the support from my Aunty beside me for my final visit to The Wheatsheaf. Tonight, I would enter the pub with a clear mind and blessed with clarity of thought after speaking to the priest. The day flew past. Looking out the window, I could see the day was coming to a close reminding me that the dark nights of autumn would soon be upon us. As the evening drew in around us, the arrival at The Wheatsheaf bore down upon us. I had previously made arrangements to all meet up at 9.30 p.m. I told my Aunty Eileen, that if she didn't mind, I would go upstairs and meditate to connect to my guides. Desperate for spiritual guidance, I hoped they could enlighten me as to what would be in store for me during the night to come.

I lit a candle and said a protection prayer to connect to my guides. I laid down on my bed in complete silence. Relaxing my body and lying perfectly still I began to unwind. It wasn't long before a connection was formed. A voice came softly but firmly to my right ear, telling me not to trust what I would see that evening. 'Be prepared Suzanne. Do not get distracted by chaos as Joseph will appear differently to what you have ever experienced before.'

'Thank you,' I whispered as I drifted into a meditation. I began receiving flashback images of Joseph dragging me down into the cellar. Frightened, I knew in my heart that this had to come to an end once and for all. I've never welcomed or wanted something as much as I wanted the end of Joseph's tyranny. I asked my guides for more insight.

'Be on your guard at all times and listen to your instincts. I am here to help you.'

For that split second, I visualized a native American standing in front of me. He was wearing his full headdress, the feathers intricately worked together. Over the ear on each side was a circle of bead-work used to fasten a handful of long feathers. The long side feathers hung loosely down to his chest and seemed to dance and float in the breeze. A small pouch hung around his neck on thin strips of leather. His eyes seemed knowing as he smiled at me. I could hear horses whinny in the distance.

For those few seconds, I felt immense peace wrapping itself around me like a comforting blanket. All too soon his image vanished. As much as I willed him to come back, he did not, but I was left breathing in fresh air with a renewed crispness. I continued to lie on my bed, knowing my guides had taken me to another plane. The sun-weathered native had come to show me that I had never been left unaided. Even though the past six weeks had been horrific, I hadn't walked it alone. This was my calling and I suspected he would become a big part of my spiritual journey. Destined to walk into The Wheatsheaf all those weeks ago, I now felt a part of a bigger plan. When my meditation came to a close, I developed a raging hunger which I hadn't felt for a long time. I needed to fuel my body before I walked back into turmoil. I knew I couldn't stand in front of Joseph on an empty stomach. It was difficult to describe how I felt after witnessing my memorable vision. I got up from my bed feeling clear-headed and knowing my guides had taken away all the worry and strain from my little shoulders. It was time to join my family downstairs.

On entering the living room, I could see Aunty Eileen sitting on the settee with the kids on her knee watching a Disney film which I had seen numerous times in the past. 'Oh God,' I said as they looked at me. 'Not another viewing of Barbie of Swan Lake.'

'Yes Mum, Aunty Eileen hasn't seen it before.'

Aunty looked at me with a twinkle in her eye and laughed. 'I have come all the way from Liverpool to watch this with my little Francesca.'

'Well,' I replied. 'At least you're all clued up on Barbie and Disney movies. I have watched them over and over again. They're the kid's favourite films.' I walked into the kitchen to see Mark was preparing a meal.

'Hi Love,' he smiled. He was busy peeling some spuds for chips and had burgers sizzling away in the oven. The smell of them cooking rekindled my ravenous appetite.

'What time is it?' Mark pointed his paring knife at the clock. 8.00 p.m.

'Oh no, I only have an hour before we head off.'

'Well, you've time to have your tea and see the kids off to bed before you shoot off to the pub. Are you ready to face him again?' He looked at me, waiting for me to crumble as the words were slipping out of my mouth.

'I am as ready as I will ever be.' I gave him a smile.

Soon, we sat down to a lovely meal which completely depleted the remainder of the time I would get to spend at home that day.

Before I knew it, I was loading up the car with the paraphernalia which I had gathered for the visual earlier that afternoon.

'Right, Aunty. Are we ready to venture into the dark and mysterious Wheatsheaf?' I let out a sigh as the inevitable was about to unfold. I said goodbye to Mark and the kids and then slowly walked towards my car with my Aunty Eileen at my side. It was extremely comforting to know there was going to be support behind me. I drove out of my estate and down the usual road that leads to The Wheatsheaf.

'Are you OK?' I glanced at her sitting on the passenger seat.

She looked at me and gave me a smile. 'Yes, I am fine.' She placed her hand over mine on the gear shift and gave it a squeeze I knew it was her way to say everything was going to work out alright. With us both in deep thought, the rest of the drive to The Wheatsheaf was deadly silent. I didn't say a word as we approached the roundabout at the bottom of the road.

'Is this the place Suzanne?' She was fidgeting in her seat as she waited for my reply.

'Yep... this is the one and only.' I turned the car and parked in my usual spot at the back of the pub. Facing the wall with the trees at the back of the waste land, I stopped the engine and stared into the wooded area. I was reminiscing back to the times when I had been here every night in the month of September. It felt like a lifetime ago. I took a deep breath.

'Right, are we ready?' I was about to open the car door when Aunty reached over to me and flung her arms around me.

'Don't be frightened Suzanne, you're not alone this time.'

I opened my arms to return the hug.

We held ourselves within the warm and safe embrace for several seconds.

'I will be fine, don't worry about me.'

We grabbed the bags from the boot and then walked slowly towards the doors that led to the lounge.

The group were waiting for me to arrive. I was welcomed with lots of smiles and hugs from them all, it was like old times again. As I introduced my Aunty Eileen to the group, I noticed there were some new faces accompanying us for the ensuing visual. I was introduced to two men named Brian and Charlie, who were Phil's friends. They were hoping they could take part in the visual. I didn't mind as long as they understood this was going to be an unpredictable night. I really couldn't complain, I'd broken my own rule and brought my Aunty along to join us. Counting heads, there were fourteen people who would witness what lay in store for me.

Sam was over the moon to see me again. 'It's good to see you all back for the final showdown.'

They laughed and joked and kept the mood light. Denise couldn't wait to comment. 'Well if it's anything like the last time you confronted Joseph, then God help us all. My arms were aching for days after you challenging him on the Ouija board.'

Phil brought the rest of the group up to speed, delving into the details of what had happened back in September. I looked at them all. There wasn't one skeptical face in the bunch. Not one person had ever doubted what had happened. I could see their dedication to me. They would all stand beside me loyally, as I fought Joseph to the bitter end.

Denise broke everyone's conversations by asking if the little girl was still in my home.

As I looked at them, there was an anticipatory silence. 'She is safe in my home until she is ready to leave. I haven't forced any pressure upon her to send her to the other side. She will go when she is good and ready.'

'Does that not scare you Suzanne?' Sam asked with concern on her face.

'No she is safe and I don't hear her all the time. Now and again, I can see her playing with the kids who are oblivious to her. I've seen her sitting in the living room when everything is quiet. She doesn't look as distressed anymore, not like she was when she was trapped in this pub. To be honest, there have been times I've wished to see her more. It's as if my motherly instinct kicks in and I worry about her wellbeing.'

'Oh well, if it's helping her to heal then she is better off where she is,' Sam said, as she rubbed my shoulder to give thanks for saving the little girl.

My mind spun back to the 15th of September. It had been a Wednesday night. I recalled the moment I clapped eyes on her standing at the top of the stairs only a few feet away from me. *My God a lot of water had passed under the bridge since then.*

Sam broke my trip down a macabre memory lane, by generously offering my Aunty and I a hot beverage before we made plans for the night.

'Yeah,' I said, 'that would be lovely.'

Being back amongst The Wheatsheaf group was like putting on your favourite old pair of jeans. Comfortable. We had been brought back together again for a final night. We talked for over an hour before I mentioned I was going to follow my normal procedure of cleansing the pub before facing him. Suddenly I felt uncomfortable, I could feel him in the room watching my every move. *Come on Suzanne, it's time to make a start.* I felt we were running out of time.

Joseph

Alarm bells were ringing in my head as I grabbed my bag and explained to the rest of the group what the procedure for the night entailed. I then walked towards the bottom of the stairs. I could hear the rest of the group close behind me. I wanted them to stay close as I didn't want anyone to feel terrified or intimidated. Chris walked beside me, I smiled at him.

'Are you ok Suzanne?'

'Yeah, I am okay Chris… just a little on edge for tonight, that's all'.

'I will be right beside you if you need me,' he said, as he opened the door. Standing on the threshold of the room, I could feel the breeze from the hole in the wall; there was a chill surrounding me. I rubbed my hands together for warmth and comfort. I was shocked to feel the daunting energy had come back so quickly.

Chris stepped into the veil of darkness of the room, and managed to switch on the light.

What the hell was that? I could see a shadow play. It was indistinct and moving about as it formed. It came to a stop at the end of the corridor between the two rooms where it slowly took the shape of a man.

'Hold on a sec Chris.' I paused to catch my breath; my heart was skipping a beat.

'What is it?' he asked with a start. I looked to see the entire group were on pins.

'I am convinced I have just seen a shadow figure walking in between the two rooms.'

'Oh fuck,' Chris pointed to the door. We all watched as the door slowly swung opened under its own steam. Mesmerized, Chris held his hand, pointing, and went quiet. The rest of the group gasped.

'What are we going to do Suzanne?' Sam's voice was barely a choked whisper. Turning around to face the group standing behind me, I was apprehensive as to what move I should make. Not only was their fear contagious, but I felt they were in danger.

'Come on, let's go.' As I walked closer towards the open door, my eyes were transfixed on the dark room. From the corner of my eye, I could see the kitchen door was also open. The room was drenched in darkness.

Standing in the doorway, a tall shadow made itself visible as it moved about in the room. I quickly moved Chris out of harm's way, and headed straight for it. The dim lights from the cookers helped to break the oppressive feeling. Looking around, I could see there were no changes to the layout since my visit a few weeks previously. As I focused on the dark corner where the spiral stairs had once been, a black shadow appeared, a mere two feet in front of me. It was Joseph. He looked aggressive as he stood there staring at me. He seemed to strain as he held himself back. My heart was beating hard, I found it hard to breath. He slowly took one deliberate step out of the darkness towards me.

'Stand your ground Suzanne,' I muttered under my breath, although I had no idea how I would accomplish this.

He leaned stiffly towards me, his upper body seemed unnaturally too far forward to maintain proper balance. Inches away from my face, he spoke with ill intent. 'I am coming for you tonight, just you wait and see.' His wretched breath sent shivers all around my body.

Oh dear God, please help me. I felt so defenseless in his presence; I became terrified. I waited to see what terrible plan he would follow for my early dispatch. He was different this time, more confident than ever and wise to the fact that my company didn't faze him. I could see he had been overly eager for me to come back and fight. Without saying a word, I stepped back from his energy, knowing he was too powerful at that moment for me to face. I was breaking inside, my mind was in a panic as a million and one thoughts, none of them wholesome, flashed one after another. Frozen to the spot, I stood and watched him draw closer towards me once more. I felt like a frightened child searching for the shelter of its mother's arms.

'You will die tonight. I have waited for your tedious, meddling soul to return, now it's time for you to die.'

The sickening vengeance in his voice knocked me back several steps, but I managed to stay on my feet. So intense was his presence, it was perfectly clear that he was out for revenge and didn't care how or when he would exact it. There was no remorse coming from this evil menace. I didn't take my eyes off him, I didn't dare.

As he jerkily stepped back, one step at a time, his evil glare continued to burn deep into my soul. He left me with one final phrase. 'You are mine tonight.' He stepped backward, without turning his back to me and melded into the darkness behind him.

My legs went to jelly and I felt I was about to faint, when Chris caught me under the arms and guided me out of the kitchen and into the room next door.

'Suzanne are you OK?' I could hear my Auntie's concerned but distant voice. I was in a tunnel, my vision was blurred and I couldn't speak a word. All I could think about were the threats he had thrown at me seconds earlier. My body was shaking with shock. As I began to recover, I lifted my head to see everyone standing around me. They looked worried from having seen me switch off and go into a trance. I was dumbfounded by Joseph's presence, I hadn't expected him to be as strong or to see the way he stood so confidently. His energy had definitely intensified; I was terrified to carry this night out, unsure what it would bring in my direction.

'I'm okay.' I was shocked to hear my own subdued voice.

'Are you sure? You look like you have seen a ghost! What happened in the kitchen?' The group were all firing their questions of concern in my direction.

I placed my head in my hands and told the group what I had just experienced. I explained how he had gained full strength and was coming for me tonight.

'Noooo,' my Aunty screamed out. 'He isn't going to hurt you Suzanne. He has done enough.'

I sat on the settee, staring at the floor, trying to think of a way to defeat him, but I was met by my own blank mind. All the plans I had made, had evaporated away when Joseph confronted me. I looked from the floor to the group.

'I will be alright.' I gave a half-hearted smile from the corners of my mouth.

'Suzanne,' Sam sat beside me and placed her arm around me. 'Come on, it's going to be okay.'

I looked at her, desperately wanting to believe her and trying to hide the fear in my face. However, it was blatantly obvious to everyone that I was terrified.

I let out a sigh, stood up and walked over to my bag. Taking out my new prayer book and the silver cross that Father McDade had given me, I spoke without confidence.

'Well… I have been through worse with Joseph, so let's see what he is going come up with next.' I didn't feel in control and felt there was something far worse than being flung down the stairs awaiting me, but I couldn't place it yet. 'Sam? Could you help me cleanse the room from top to bottom?'

'Yes of course,' she said.

We got everything ready, incense, prayer book and sage to smudge the rooms as we went along. I was just about to begin, when a knock came at the door. We all jumped, as we weren't expecting anyone. The door quickly opened.

'Hello,' came a man's voice.

'Hi,' I answered back, sounding confused.

We all turned around to see him standing in the middle of the room.

'What the hell are you doing in here?' He directed his shouting at my Aunty and Chris as everyone stood in awkward amazement. 'Who the hell are you?' It was surreal to see this unknown man hurling abuse at us.

'I am Suzanne.' He looked over at me in disgust.

'And I'm James. Are you the so called psychic who has put a gaping hole in the wall of my pub?'

'Yes,' I nodded nervously. I began to explain why there was a hole in the wall, but he wasn't about to let me get a word in edgewise.

'I am one of the partners of this pub.'

I interrupted the man's cocky outburst and tried to calm his ire.

'Well I am not impressed,' he said as he pushed past me and walked towards the far wall. 'Look at all the dust on my furniture. Are you going to clean up all this bloody mess?' He turned to glare at me.

'Look, I think we have got off on the wrong foot.' As I talked to him about the happenings which had taken place in his pub, I could see he was beginning to listen to my explanation. 'I was unaware of another partner involved in the pub or I would have asked for your permission to carry out digging for the little girl.'

'I wonder if Phil ever once thought of calling to let me know what the hell was going on?'

I tried to explain how we had been caught up in the moment, Phil included, but James didn't let me finish.

Striking through my sentence, he clearly wasn't interested in what I had to say. 'Phil has some bloody explaining to do.'

I didn't have to be a medium to pick up on the fact that the man hated what was going on.

'I have just flown back from Cyprus. I live out there in the summer months and I heard through the grapevine about what's happened here in the pub.'

I couldn't help but think what a pretentious prick he was. I could fully understand why Phil hadn't clued him in.

'Sorry for being so short with you, I wasn't expecting the room to be like a builder's yard when I walked in.' His voice was filled with sarcasm.

Sam came rushing towards me and tried to calm James down enough so that maybe he would, at the very least, hear our side of the story.

'Alright Sam… you have been a good worker over the months, could you possibly vouch for this woman's actions.'

'Oh yes,' she exclaimed. 'She has helped us try to bring peace back into the pub.'

He sighed as he looked around the room.

I was sitting on edge, as it was his decision on whether or not to let this night go ahead.

'Okay Susan,' he said as I cringed at the name he had given me. The man was a waste of air to me, it wasn't worth wasting my time to correct it to Suzanne. 'I will let you stay as long as you don't go digging for gold in the walls.'

I nodded as he turned on his highly polished heel, about to walk out of the room. James was nearly to the door when it opened again and a stocky built man popped his head through the doorway. I looked at the rest of the group and James. It became clear no one had any idea who this man was. Everyone looked confused.

'Friend of yours James?' He rolled his eyes at me.

'No,' he answered in a sharp tone. 'I've never seen him before.'

With having met two unknown men in the space of a few short minutes, I was feeling guarded, the stocky built man looked very suspicious to me. I felt my senses sharpen.

James turned to leave, he'd obviously had enough of the likes of us. I watched him hastily walk towards the door, throwing a glare at me on his way. However, the second man wouldn't move aside to let him out. James' face changed to confusion as he watched the man staring intently at the hole in the wall, unwilling to move to the side to allow him to pass by.

'Are you okay?' I asked the new arrival.

He looked at me, disgruntled that I had broken his concentration. 'Oh yeah… I am fine. What are all the bricks for?' he asked in a monotone manner.

I looked at the rest of the group with a perplexed look on my face. 'It's nothing really, why do you ask?' I could see he wouldn't take his eyes off the rubble piles.

'Do you know anything about bricks?'

Looking at this man and noting his build, I could have easily made him out to be a construction worker. After a rather extended awkward pause, he answered. 'Me?' he pointed to himself, then shook his head. 'No I am a fisherman by trade.'

'Oh right.' It seemed I was having a one- sided conversation with him, I could see he wasn't the type to chat a lot.

'How did you come to know we were in this room?' Again came the extended wait for a reply.

'Well, I was on my way out of the gent's toilets, when something drew me to this room.' He looked blankly at me. 'I am Kevin,' he said, returning his eyes to the pile of bricks lying next to the hole in the fireplace wall. 'What are you looking for in the wall?' he looked at me briefly then reverted his eyes back to the red slabs on the floor. I felt he was eager to walk over and touch them.

'Oh nothing much really,' I said as I stared at him. I looked around to the other group members, they were stood in silence. I could see they were as gobsmacked as I was, that this man had appeared from nowhere.

'I know you're lying,' he glared straight at me.

Possession

Kevin's arrival had now taken us down a more sinister road. He held his angry gaze at me and then seemed to go into a trance. He then spoke mechanically. 'If you want to find her, look for the green bricks.'

'What?' I asked in amazement, but he had already turned away, once again mesmerized by the brick piles. Slowly, I repeated what he had just said to myself.

He then spoke again. 'If you want to find the child, look for the green paint.'

*What green pain*t? My heart stopped along with my breathing. Standing in the middle of the room, we all had our eyes firmly fixed on the newcomer. Not one of us could believe what they had just heard coming out of his mouth. He stepped further into the room and walked towards the rubble piles. He dropped to his knees in front of the pile and then began to lay his hands on each and every timeworn piece. He hesitated after picking each one up, as if he was channeling through to find some energy within the bricks and mortar. I was in shock; I tapped Sam on the shoulder and in a hushed whisper, asked her if she had ever seen this man in the pub before. She looked at me and shook her head.

'No, never Suzanne,' she whispered back.

'What do you mean about the green paint?' I questioned him abruptly.

He looked at me as if I was stupid, a brick tightly held in his left hand.

'It's Elizabeth and Joseph.'

'My God.' I quickly put my mouth in check. *How the hell does he know this information?*

He turned his head and began to put the bricks into separated piles on the floor.

My Aunty Eileen has never been shy to lend a helping hand. She was more than capable of looking after herself in a tricky situation. I wasn't a bit surprised to see her bend down beside him to help Kevin sort out the bricks. She handed each one to him, and as he held each it in his hand, he would say yes or no. I came to the conclusion that he was connecting to something within the 'yes' bricks and not in the others. Two separate stacks began to grow on the floor. He then began to come out with more information. He spoke of a group of men fighting in the back of the pub, then spewed out dates and times. I was shocked at his ability to recall information it had taken me weeks to uncover,.

'This is unbelievable,' I commented to the group, but they didn't utter a word. I asked Sam and James again, if they were absolutely positive they had never met this man before.

By this point, James was looking absolutely lost, he had squelched his attitude with me and asked me what was going on. I filled James in as quickly as possible.

'Sam could you do me a favour and go and ask Phil and the rest of the staff if they know who Kevin is and if they have seen him before?' She readily agreed and walked out of the room with James following close on her heels.

'Chris could you help me by filming this, maybe he has the answer we need.'

Everyone was dumbfounded by Kevin's sudden appearance. Witnessing this man coming out of thin air, then talking about the little girl in the wall had set us all on edge. I jumped out of my skin as Kevin grabbed my arm.

'Do you have a notepad and pen?'

I rummaged through my bags and found both items. I quickly handed them over to him.

He bent down and began to draw the woman he was seeing within his vision. He then flung the paper through air and snarled. 'That's what she looks like.' Returning to sorting out the bricks, he began muttering under his breath.

I bent down to help my Aunty sort out the bricks. *Don't break his concentration, help him stay focused.* I was eagerly awaiting more information. What he had already come out with was remarkable. It was unbelievable to witness the similarities to what I had previously discovered.

He described the kitchen as his office. The ladies who had died in the pub were mentioned, as were the screams from the children who had their lives ruined by him. He kept on referring to Joseph as him, not wanting to say his name.

I couldn't understand why. I looked at my Aunty as she passed each brick to Kevin. He continued with the yes and no sorting. With each new piece, he became more and more agitated. After a few minutes of this sorting process had passed, I went to grab some candles from my bag. Auntie's words stopped me in my tracks.

'It's him Suzanne.' She looked like she had seen a ghost.

'What are you talking about?' She slowly lifted her hand and pointed over to Kevin.

'He has stopped sorting, he seems to be in a trance, his lip keeps curling up into a snarl.' He had stopped picking up the bricks and was staring straight ahead. I heard a soft growl and watched my Aunty move quickly away from him. She came over to me. 'Suzanne, I am telling you now that Kevin has changed, it isn't him anymore.'

I quickly turned to see what my Aunty was trying to describe. I looked around the room to see some of the group all huddled up in the corner. They could sense something was wrong. I slowly walked over to see Kevin bent down and paused over his 'yes' pile. He was staring vacantly, as if he had been taken over by a presence.

'Are you okay?' There was no response. I apprehensively walked closer to him and repeated my question. 'Are you okay?' I asked with a quiver in my voice. Unable to answer, he sat there firmly in a trance. 'KEVIN!!!'

He jumped and gave me a snarl.

As he looked up at me, I could see the changes my Aunty had tried to describe. *Oh shit! What the hell am I going to do now? Joseph has taken over this man's body.* I shouted his name repeatedly, I was adamant to get him to respond. 'Kevin speak to me right now!!'

'You think you're so fucking clever don't you?'

As the words left his lips, the walls of the room came drawing close and my body began to shake. What am I going to do? What am I going to do? The question kept repeating in my head. None too soon, I heard the voices from my guides, telling me to get out of the room and get Kevin downstairs as it was time to face Joseph. *Don't panic Suzanne,* I tried to console my troubled mind and heart. *Just get everyone downstairs.*

'Right everyone! Get yourselves down to the safe zone asap. Chris, I need your help to bring Kevin to the safe zone.'

He stood there and shook his head. I could see he was more than a little bit wary of touching Kevin, but I needed us both to lead him down the stairs.

We waited until everyone had cleared the room, before we made a move to grab the new arrival, but he suddenly stood up and looked at us both, glaring with evil in his eyes.

' Suzanne, are we going to be able to take him down the stairs?'

'We have no other choice Chris.' I walked over to Kevin and gently grabbed his arm. He shrugged my hand away and then walked towards the door. I watched in horror as he quickly stomped down the corridor, then started down the stairs.

Denise and Sam could hear the steps coming towards them.

I raced down the hallway. 'He is coming towards you.' I could hear the groups' expletives as they gasped in a panic. 'Whatever you do don't let Kevin leave this pub!' I screamed whilst trying to catch up to him. I was panicking; I couldn't protect the group who were down in the safe zone.

He sped down the stairs with me flying two feet behind him. Reaching the bottom, I looked over to see the group all huddled up at the back wall in the safe zone.

Kevin had moved quickly. I spotted him standing with his back towards me, trying to open the front door. He was scratching at its black paint trying to find a gap. I walked towards him. 'Kevin!' There was no response. I shouted again with added volume. 'KEVIN!!'

He slowly turned to face me. I was petrified inside. There directly in front of me stood the human form of Joseph. I needed to be especially careful this time. He was ready to pounce and I would be the first victim in the line of fire. Apprehensive to take another step towards him, I felt the fear rush through my veins. 'Kevin!'.

He stood there and didn't murmur a single word. His lips curled and snarled at me in disgust. He checked the seating area in front of him and sat in the corner next to the front door. He sat with his head bowed down, not looking like the man that I had met less than an hour before. I noticed his facial features had changed.

'Kevin!' I said in a sharp tone of voice. All I could hear were astonished whispers from the rest of the group. As I turned my head to my right, I could see everyone's heads peering through the little glass panels surrounding the safe zone.

'Everyone stay there. Don't... fucking... move from the safe zone,' I reminded them. I heard Sam whisper.

'Don't fucking worry, we won't.'

My hands lay heavy on the table that was in between Kevin and I. 'I know you can hear me.' As I took a deep breath I could feel Chris' presence standing right behind me as he filmed us. We both seemed to sense that it would be unwise to make any sudden moves, just in case it riled the man up like a cornered animal. I bent my head down and let out a sigh, then looked at the transformation. He was staring at Joseph's corner which was situated behind me a few feet away in the darkness. As he glared at me, it confirmed that his facial features had indeed changed. I could see Joseph was taking up his true form.

'Yes you heard me.' He scowled, but didn't retaliate, he just sat there and snarled. 'You're a fucking pain in my arse.' He started to move as if he was going to get up and knock me into next week, but he seemed weak and uncoordinated. It was taking Joseph some getting used to; he hadn't been bound by a physical body in a very long time.

'I am going to kill you,' he shouted.

I could hear gasps and screams coming from the group as he abruptly stood up. I felt defenseless against his threats. I watched him move slowly towards the stairs. *That's it I've had enough!* I ran after him and pulled at his arm.

'You're not going anywhere you dickhead!' I jumped in front of him and pushed him backwards towards his chair. With a final shove I managed to sit him down in the seat he had been wedged in a few seconds earlier. I could feel he was gaining strength and coordination. Glancing at Chris and the others, I could see they were dumbfounded by witnessing what was happening before their eyes.

'Chris quickly run upstairs and get my bag, please hurry, we don't have much time, he has nearly completed the transition into Joseph. Everybody be careful and alert, he is about to erupt.'

It was then that an idea came into my head. I would need to drag his ass into the safe zone and draw him out of Kevin. At that point I could give him a non-return ticket to hell. I needed time to prepare for the cleanse as well as keeping my eyes on him and protecting the group. Feeling overwhelmed, I began panicking inside, as all three tasks were of equal importance. I did not know which direction to turn to.

Chris raced down the stairs with my bag. I pulled the zip open and desperately grabbed for my prayer book which was lying on the top as if it was calling out to me. As I began to recite the prayers listed on the pages, I looked at Kevin. He was sitting there laughing at my pathetic attempts to dispose of him. My voice was wobbly with nerves as I asked the higher powers and archangels to come and descend on Joseph. His laughter rubbed my last nerve raw. I snapped.

'I wouldn't laugh if I were you.' I leaned closer to him testing my own fears. 'It's only a matter of time for you. Soon you will be laughing on the other side of your face when I knock your block off your shoulders.'

He shook his head and snickered. 'You will die tonight little girl.'

'Sam prepare for a protection prayer in the safe zone please.'

'Okay Suzanne, I've got the book.'

I could hear the nerves in her voice. I had to be one step ahead of Joseph and stay in complete control. *He is clever, but I know he has met his match with me. Soon I would be kicking him into oblivion. He won't forget me in a hurry.* Standing within arm's reach of him, we bantered back and forth, I gave as good as I got. We were in constant eye contact all the way through.

I admit he had caught me off guard with possessing Kevin. Remembering my guides warning about distractions, I put two and two together. This man had been sent for that exact purpose. Lighting a candle, I asked for help and protection from the archangels.

I jumped as he stood up and walked towards Joseph's corner. *Was this to divert me from the prayers?* Standing in the darkness, watching my every move, he tried to distract me with his feeble intimidation tactics. His shoulders were hunched and his body seemed poised to attack like a wild cat.

As the minutes passed, I could see he was looking more and more like Joseph. His body frame seemed bigger and his jawline had bulged out to take the square shape of the evil entity. I became transfixed by the physical changes appearing in front of me. Attempts at intimidation may have been feeble minutes earlier, but now they were pretty damn convincing. He was now towering in height. I was reminded of my visions, the same image, but this time appearing in a physical body.

I flinched as he moved again, this time it was like the vision I had had a few days previously. He began walking towards me, every step he took increased my heart rate until it felt as if it was beating out of my chest.

'This is it,' I said under my breath. 'He is coming for me.' The evil of Joseph's eyes had completely transformed within Kevin's. The transformation was now complete. I placed my hands over my mouth in shock; I could hear the group's screams and gasps at every move he made. I let out a sigh of relief when he suddenly stopped a few feet away from me. Everyone went still and silent.

'What's going on Suzanne, this is scaring the hell out of us!?' Phil's voice cut through the morbid silence. I wouldn't turn to talk to Phil, I was that frightened of taking my eyes off Kevin.

'It's OK everyone, don't set foot out of the safe zone.'

'Oh believe us we won't,' Phil shook his head. It was the only safe place in the entire pub and they were more than happy staying within it.

Still filming, Chris remained beside me and asked from behind the camera if I thought Kevin would be okay.

'Yes,' I said with a not so convinced tone in my voice.

I was uncertain for Kevin's wellbeing. He had walked away and was now standing back in Joseph's corner. It was time to seize the opportunity to speak with the group. Without delay, I made my way into the safe zone.

'Right, I don't have much time, but we need to all be aware of what's about to happen. This is my plan. We need to bring him within the safe zone.' As I looked from face to face of the people who had supported me so loyally, I instantly could feel their fear. They hadn't missed that I had mentioned Joseph and the safe zone in the same sentence. 'We need Joseph in the circle for my guides to draw his energy away from his physical hostage, or Kevin will be in grave danger. So, could we move the chairs around to form a circle so that I can sit him in the middle and begin the cleanse?' I heard him moving about in the darkness. Spotting his shadow shifting was one of the most frightening experiences I've ever had. He was trying to slip himself through the wall leading to the corridor. Repeatedly he tried to glide through the wall, thumping eerily as Kevin's body stopped him each time. Suddenly it dawned on me that he couldn't escape. Now posed within another man's body, there was no flitting in and out of the walls. He could no longer slip where he wanted to. Manifesting in random dark spaces to scare me half to death was no longer an option when inhabiting a solid body.

I ran towards him yelling with rage. 'Joseph, you can't walk through walls and sneak around; you have possessed Kevin's body you numskull.'

He turned and raised his arms as if he were waving someone toward him and as he did so, I could feel he was no longer alone. *Oh God, he has brought the other dark energies through with him and they are about to ambush me!* Time was now extremely short.

'Right, before you think you can drag me off to hell, I need to make a suggestion.' I yanked his arm and attempted to drag him into the safe zone.

'Leave me!' he shouted aggressively. Brushing my hand away from his arm as though he was swatting away a fly, he then walked off in big strides and disappeared into the corridor.

I felt deflated. *What in God's name am I going to do?* Tension was gripping me tight. The group were on edge as they busied themselves arranging the tables to prepare for Joseph's entry to the safe zone. I had tested the water with my first attempt on getting him into the circle. I knew this was going to be a lot more difficult than what I had anticipated. I needed a hell of a lot more strength to get me through this and pull him into the safe zone.

In resignation, I lifted my hands and made let-it-settle-down motions. I decided to leave him for a couple of minutes as we prepared for the cleanse. By that time, my frustration levels had hit the top shelf. I didn't really care what or where he was, until I was ready to bring him into my domain. I needed time to reassure the group that everything was in control; no matter what I would happily lay my life on the line for everyone in that room.

Standing in the safe zone, I watched the group organizing their seating arrangements. I noticed there were two seats left unoccupied on either side of the chair picked out for Joseph to sit his ass on. I noticed Phil and Sam had picked a seat next to the empty chairs. With a nervous laugh I brought it to their attention.

'I would dearly love to be the person to sit next to Kevin and watch one of you fine people draw him out,' I laughed. 'But unfortunately, I am the person to stand in the line of fire.'

It wasn't surprising to see that they were all dubious regarding sitting next to Kevin. Noticing their frightened faces, their eyes went from one person to the next waiting for someone else to volunteer to sit within the energy of Joseph. After a prolonged silence, Chris handed the camera to another team member and silently took one of the empty seats. Phil stood and took the other chair. I smiled at them both. I became emotional at the show of bravery as they volunteered to sit in the circle's empty chairs.

'I promise that neither of you will get hurt during tonight's visual. Whatever you both do, please remember, don't feed him any show of weakness or glimpses of your lives. The clever bastard can read your mind and use it against you both.'

I moved closer and gave them both a hug. I didn't want anyone to feel the pain I had been carrying over the past few weeks, but I felt certain that this was the only way I could defeat him once and for all.

We broke away from our embrace and I stepped into my place. We were all ready to lure Joseph into my domain.

I picked up my silver cross which I had received as a gift from Father

McDade. As I held it in my hands, a warm and comforting feeling enveloped me. I was relieved that I was now in the company of higher powers. They had answered my prayers.

The Motley Trio

Sam had prepared a little table beside the fireplace behind me. She had become indispensable during my time at The Wheatsheaf.

'Thank you Sam.'

She nodded and smiled.

I lit incense and closed my eyes, placing my hand over the smoking flame, asking my guides to smudge my aura and keep my energy in white light at all times.

After checking the circle for the final time, I mentally noted that I had ample space to watch every move Kevin made.

'Before we start to call him into the circle,' Sam asked in a concerned tone of voice. 'My fear is he will kick off and hurt one of us.'

I glanced at Sam with a quick smile. 'I don't know if that's his intention tonight.' I looked into every one of their faces. It was obvious that they were dubious about the whole idea. I smiled at them all. 'We will have to cross that bridge when we come to it.' I wouldn't have expected anything less of Joseph, he certainly would relish trapping us all in the midst of his shady games.

'One thing I know for certain is that my name is at the top of his list of people to hurt and maim. He has highlighted it. He has underlined it. He has placed a star next to Suzanne. I really doubt he has the want or the motive to hurt any of you, it's me he wants.'

They all burst out laughing. It was good to break the tension.

I reassured everyone that this visual would be the final visual. I would draw the curtains closed on The Wheatsheaf misadventure. 'I know this looks daunting at this moment in time,' I said as my voice began to break, 'In the end, we can always look back and say that we were the chosen ones to stand and defeat this monster. It's all noted upstairs you know. All the pain and lack of sleep, the worry and the fear, all noted upstairs.'

They all looked totally confused until I pointed heavenward to the ceiling. Once again the moment had been lightened, our laughter was a brief respite from thinking about what we were about to go through together. A terrifying ordeal awaited us that night. I could honestly have said, that the group's sense of humour was about the only thing that had kept me going through those traumatic weeks. Reality kicked in when I realized the group hadn't cracked any jokes, puns and one liners like they normally did. They had been sombre and inwardly silent since the beginning of the evening.

Propping my prayer book open, I began to cleanse the safe zone by asking my guides to fill the little space we were working in with love and light. I was ready to walk into the darkness at the entrance to the corridor. As I entered the darkened area, I couldn't see a hand in front of me. I picked up on the sound of Joseph whispering in the middle of the corridor. Fear built inside me, not from Joseph's mutterings, but from who he was directing them to. My heart stopped when I realized that three other dark energies whom I'd encountered throughout the traumatizing nights at The Wheatsheaf, were whispering back. I was apprehensive to go any further into the pitch black corridor to extract Joseph. Sadly, I knew I had to put myself at risk in order to drag him to the safe zone.

This is going to be impossible. I tried to shake off my defeatist thoughts as I began to take slow child-size footsteps. As the darkness engulfed me, the sounds of the men's whispers grew in volume. I could now make out snippets of their conversation as I neared them.

'Right gov.' I recognized Paddy's voice instantly. 'I will grab her by her mangy hair and drag her to the floor.' They sniggered amongst themselves. During my painfully slow walk down the corridor, my eyes began to adjust to the pitch black. *Thank God for small mercies.* I was a couple of feet away when the temperature dropped dramatically. I knew I was close to my nemesis.

'Joseph,' I shouted. Immediately the corridor was filled with stomping footsteps speedily approaching from behind me. I didn't need to turn around, I knew it was Kevin. As the footsteps sped up, I could hear him laughing. When he was close enough for me to hear his raspy breathing, I finally turned and looked behind me. He marched towards me at great speed. I tried to brace myself firmly to the floor and closed my eyes for a fraction of a second. I was preparing to be pushed and thrown around the pub with great force and bad intent.

'I've had about enough of you little girl,' he shouted. Since being introduced to the spectres of The Wheatsheaf, I had lost track of the number of times I'd had an entity come within my intimate space to breathe their foul exhalations in my face. The total was about to have another added to it. Kevin stopped predictably, but intimidatingly, inches away from my face. I could feel the deep cold of his atmospheric presence evaporating the air from my lungs. I tightened my grip on the silver cross in my right hand. I prayed over and over silently to myself. Gasps from the group behind me seemed distant. They had vacated their chairs in the circle to come to the edge of the safe zone to watch what we all secretly hoped would be a once in a lifetime event. With relief, the physical hiding I'd expected didn't come to fruition. He sneered at me as he stared me up and down in a deviant manner, stopping only to stare straight into my eyes. He was trying to use Kevin's body to intimidate me. I felt as though he was beginning to feel inferior in the body of another. The more I looked at him leaning over me, the less of the real man appeared. I couldn't see a single glimpse of him within the eyes, he was Joseph through and through. I watched as he continued to struggle with his intimidation routine. This scenario would have been laughable in any other situation, but to me it was another breakthrough. I knew in my mind I was ready to face him.

Reaching deep, for any remaining shreds of bravery, I made a split-second decision. I pushed him as hard as I could. The element of surprise caught him off guard as I grabbed his muscular arm and pulled him forward with all my might, step by step into the safe zone. It was obvious he hadn't completely mastered the physical attributes of Kevin's body as I slammed him down on the chair. He was clearly taken aback by my actions.

I called for Sam to recite the prayers I'd given her earlier. Everyone in the group sat in absolute silence, fully attentive to the matters at hand. It was now time for a bit of my own brand of intimidation.

'And I've had about enough of you too,' I shouted at him within inches of his face. I raised my hands to my forehead and leaned towards him to send the same vibes he had given me seconds earlier. 'Just because you are in a body now, doesn't mean you can't be defeated.' I paced back and forth in front of him. 'Oh... and another thing,' I shouted, leaning in close to his face once again. 'If you are out for revenge against me,' I shook my head and twisted my face in a sarcastic manner before continuing. 'Don't forget that I see you as nothing more than a bit of shit on the bottom of my shoe. What a waste of shit!' My comment to Joseph was met with cheers and a loud 'Hear! Hear!' From the group.

'It's a damn shame isn't it Joseph? If you had not acted like a monster in life, I wouldn't have needed to seek out the truth about your perverted deeds after your death. You don't know when to give up the ghost,' I laughed at him. 'Do you Joseph?' He stood up and glared at me. I pressed my hands down on his shoulders. 'And where the hell do you think you're going? SIT DOWN YOU HORRIBLE PRICK!' He composed himself enough to push my hand away from him and walked into the middle of the lounge.

I took a quick opportunity to stretch out my spine and shrug off the tension from my neck and shoulders. I placed my hands on my legs and arched my back. It had been refreshing to have let out so much pent up frustration, especially venting it against the cause himself. I needed to keep up the momentum, recess was over.

Aunty grabbed my hand and whispered. 'It was such a brave thing to see, you tackling him earlier on Suzanne.' She quickly gave me an impromptu hug. I could see she was fascinated by the goings on and fully enjoyed taking part in the last visual. 'Can I ask? Why does Joseph always stand near the seating area?'

As I looked into the lounge, it suddenly dawned on me that this was the first time Aunty or anyone in the group for that matter, had ever been able to see Joseph in any way shape or form. Over the past few weeks, they had heard unexplained noises or witnessed objects flying across the room. They had felt and sensed quite a lot of things, but they had never been able to witness his actions before. They had always been involved, but only by my insight and passing words.

'It's just Joseph,' I said with a shrug. 'That's what he does?' I couldn't take the time to explain anything at that moment, I would discuss it on the way home later. My mind was transfixed on the battle ahead. 'Phil and Chris could you please bring him back into the circle?'

'What?' Phil's face was a picture as he questioned what I had asked of him. He shook his head as he stood up accompanied by Chris. I could see they didn't want to go near him; I couldn't hardly blame them. Joseph was just as much of an aberration in death as he had been in life. Phil ran out of the safe zone with Chris a few steps behind him. I could see Joseph was reluctant to return into my domain, pushing away his escorts.

'Come on Joseph,' I nodded my head in a beckoning motion at the circle.

I rubbed my eyes and shook my head to ground myself back into the present. Three shadows appeared out of the corridor at the bottom of the lounge. I instantly knew they were ready to team up against me and possibly the group members. Watching them as they shifted themselves into the middle of the lounge, I realized they were only a few feet away from Phil and Chris. Instinctively, I knew they were about to make a beeline for them. Darting out of the safe zone, I aimed for the three menacing spirits who Joseph had formed and moulded under his evil control. *Oh no you don't.* At a full run, I cut through the freezing cold presences. I wasn't going to allow any one of my loyal group to be victimized by their threats. Hell bent, I ran at Paddy and his two cronies. I felt a cold pain cut across my arm as Paddy threw a swipe at me. Phil and Chris managed to manhandle Joseph back into the center of the circle. My arm began to burn. Looking down in the darkness I could see blood appearing as an inky stain. There were gashes across my upper arm, each one accompanied by burning pain. The bleeding was quickening, I could feel its wet stickiness trickling down to my forearm. I was distracted by the pain that the menacing, evil trio had inflicted on me. My guides quickly whispered. 'He is playing you like a fiddle, it's a ruse, go back quickly to the safe zone. He wants to distract you from protecting the group, to create an opportunity to hurt the group members. Hurry! Get back he is going to attack one of the group.'

As I turned I could see them all sitting in their chairs, waiting for me to take the lead. *'Oh God no, this is one of his plans to split us up and attack.* I ran back as quick as I could and resumed my position, stood over Joseph in my original spot. My heart was pounding so hard I couldn't talk, I needed a few seconds to calm down. Placing my opposite hand over the gashes to stop the bleeding, I became bewildered. My arm was dry. Looking down, there were no gashes. Joseph had added another party trick to his arsenal of distractions, one that nearly had caused me to make a devastating error.

'Thank you for bringing him to the safe zone.' I looked at Phil and Chris. *The next time he darts off into the lounge, I will have to be the one to bring him back.* My guides' advice had saved an ordeal from unfolding. In those split seconds, they had saved me and more than likely had averted a catastrophe.

As I looked at him sitting a few feet away, I could see the effect he was having on the group as they sat near to his icy energy. They all looked uncomfortable, squirming in their seats. He was sitting in a slumped position with his arms crossed like a defiant child. While he watched my every move, his face changed from anger to looking amused. He laughed in my face. I bit back again.

'Soooo… I see you have brought your so called mates along with you tonight.' The smile disappeared from his face as he glared at me. He'd obviously hoped I hadn't noticed.

'Fuck off you little bitch.'

I let out a sigh and shrugged my shoulders. My hands tightened around the objects I was holding, the silver cross in my right hand and a pendulum in my left.

'Well the old wife's tale goes like this.' I took my time, arching my back in a stretch to portray my nonchalance. I leaned in close to look him straight in the face. 'Sticks and stones may break my bones,' I hesitated. 'But names will never hurt me.' I raised my eyebrows at him and shrugged his threat off my shoulders. There was no way on God's earth I was going to crumble in front of him.

'Oh, I nearly forgot. I have a special message for you Joseph.' I could see I had his attention. 'It's from the little girl I saved. You remember her Joseph, you know, the one you murdered? Jessica? There's also messages from the rest of the lost souls that I sent on a few days ago, surely you remember them as well Joseph. They send their love. They have found peace in heaven. Oh yes, before I forget, they did say… and I quote their exact message to you, go to hell. I agree with each one of those tortured souls, that's the best place for you.' I stepped back and waited for his reply. He bent his head down and muttered.

'You bitch.'

'What did you say Joseph? I couldn't hear your cowardly mutterings'. He stood up fiercely and stepped closer towards me.

'I said you're a bitch.'

'I have an inclination that those are the only words you can come out with.' I stepped closer to him and pushed him back down on his seat. 'Joseph, Joseph, I'm trying to have a battle of wits with you, but it's impossible, you are sadly sooooooooooo unarmed.'

I quickly turned my head to see Chris and Phil both sitting with their heads down shivering and crying like children. They had become completely intimidated by his presence. Chris raised his head when he noticed I was looking at him. 'I am okay, I don't know what the hell is the matter with me,' he sniffled.

'It's okay,' I replied trying to reassure him.

He nodded and placed his head back down. My heart was aching for them both, but I knew if I was to break the circle at this crucial moment we would risk Kevin's well-being. I secretly hoped he wouldn't be scarred by being privy to evil memories. It was vital Joseph remained within the safe zone until I could find the right time to crack his resolve and draw him out of Kevin. Remembering back to my guides' kind words, 'Don't get distracted, watch his every move.' It was imperative that I concentrate on him and nothing else.

Once again, I asked my guides for protection as I opened up my prayer book to recite the first line. I turned to page 15, Psalm 23, "As I walk through the valley of death..." I was shouting from the top of my lungs, unwilling to show him any fear. He shot up and walked directly in front of my face. His sudden move caught every one of us off guard. The group screamed, some of them jumped off their chairs.

He was breathing heavily, like an angered bull ready to charge. I froze, torn between disguising my fear and figuring out my next move. Just as I feared I may become airborne, he turned his head to look towards the cellar door. It was only a brief reprieve, he looked back to me. His domineering glare was now firmly transfixed in my direction.

'I could see through his soul,' he snarled as he made reference to Kevin.

I gasped and jumped back fearing I'd overstepped my mark with this entity.

Locking his cheekbones with anger and without breaking our eye contact, he stepped back and walked toward the dark energies standing outside the cellar door.

'Oh my God,' Sam cried as she watched him walk towards the other end of the lounge. She quickly turned and let out a guttural emotional cry. She had held it in for far too long and was unable to contain it any longer.

I felt I was losing control of the situation. We were all showing fear and feeding Joseph's insatiable appetite for weakness.

'Okay everyone, take a breath.' I let out a sigh and felt tears welling up in my eyes. Rubbing my forehead to give myself some comfort, I realized I had to regain control of the visual. I had to think fast on my feet. 'What am I going to do?' I muttered under my breath. As I watched his shape skulking by the cellar door, I began to hear the whispering amongst Joseph and his motley trio. It was hard to make out the three dark shadows surrounding Joseph as they prepared to ambush me. I knew I had to take time to pull the group back together.

'I know this might be one of the most difficult things I've ever asked you all to do. We must put our reactions in check. We are breaking down and showing our fears and emotions. We are feeding the very beast we need to starve. I am just as at fault as you are. Emotions are a tough thing to contain. I think we should break away for...' I didn't get to finish before Phil stopped me.

'Suzanne!! He's on the move.'

I could hear a quiver in his voice. Phil stood up from his chair and pointed to Joseph. We all could see he was aiming towards the corner. Joseph was standing in the darkness, watching us watching him.

'Oh Suzanne,' Denise whispered as she came over and grabbed my hand. 'This is serious, it's so frightening, I've never seen anything like this in my life.' She was rightfully frightened as were the rest of the group. It was leaving a strain on all their faces. I looked at Chris and Phil, they were visibly shaking, trembling inside and out. I reached for the bottle of water in my handbag and handed it to them.

'Do you need to take a step out?' I looked at them both. They both shook their heads.

'No, I am going to see this through,' Chris said adamantly as he finished off his share of the water. He shrugged his shoulders back and then shook out the tension.

'This is very difficult. I hate to see you both going through this, but please hang in there, it won't be for much longer.'

'Okay are we ready?'

Chris answered a yes for them both.

I shot out of the safe zone and ran towards Kevin. Joseph and his motley crew had nestled their evil presence within the walls of the lounge. It had only taken them a few hours and the atmosphere of The Wheatsheaf had returned to the way it had been back in September. 'No more gallivanting about now Joseph.' I pushed through the three dark energies and stopped directly in front of him. Astounded, he stood motionless. I grabbed his arm with all my might and dragged and pushed him back to the safe zone. I didn't mess about; I knew full well I would only have one shot with the benefit of surprise. Dragging Joseph, I quickly turned and pushed him onto the chair. Feeling confident, I turned my back towards him. 'Right,' I said glaring over my shoulder. 'Let's start again.' I nodded to Sam to begin to reading out the next prayer.

'As the Lord is my shepherd...'

I looked at Chris and Phil as Sam read on. They were on the verge of breaking down into their second trembling fit. I worried for them, no one had much control left. Our nerves were shattered. I leaned over to Kevin's face.

'Come on Joseph.'

He looked deep into my soul, shaking his head in disgust.

'Let's dance.' Stepping back, I let the pendulum which had been tucked within my right hand slip through my fingers on its chain until it swung in front of him. Joseph turned his head away and looked at the floor. I could see he was not amused. His body language was defiant. He had his shoulders shrugged up and his arms crossed. 'Watch this Joseph' he looked at me and snarled. 'Say goodbye to your trinity of puppets.'

Before I closed my eyes to proceed, I scanned the faces of the fourteen onlookers. Their eyes were all firmly looking at me. I don't think they were willing to look in Joseph's direction. Our steely resolve and bravery levels were running close to empty. I closed my eyes and asked my guides to surround the pub with love and light as Sam recited the prayers on the list I had given her.

'Draw out the evil that haunts this pub!' I shouted out at top volume.

Standing in the middle of the safe zone, I lifted my arm to hold the pendulum freely in front of me. There was no hesitation of movement as the pendulum began to spin immediately. Within seconds it was spinning forcefully. The weight of it as it swung began to pull my right hand down, the crystal attached to the bottom was swinging so fiercely that I began to struggle to control it. An overwhelming heaviness seemed to be drawing my energy into the pendulum. Just as I feared I may not be able to manage its power, a bright light appeared within the middle of the crystal. My heart was pounding in my chest as I began to feel the magnitude of black energy around me. Intense forces seemed to ooze from the walls. Joseph had literally scarred The Wheatsheaf with his inhuman deeds. All I could do, was close my eyes and ask my guides for strength as I tightened my hand around the pendulums chain. The spinning dowser had picked up so much speed that it began making a whistling sound.

I then visualized a bright ball of love and light hovering in front of my face and asked the energy from within it to dissolve all the past pain recorded in the fabric of the building itself. I then went on to ask it to release the pub from anything evil. At that point, as the light ball moved, I could see it circling around me and the dowser. The negative powers began to shift, as the light filled with positivity and light evaporated any dark energy that stood in its way.

A putrid smell now assaulted my nostrils, the moist fumes of mildew began hitting the back of my throat. It was wafting in from my right hand side. I quickly opened my eyes to see the three dark energies being pulled into the dowser. With every molecule of dark energy entering the pendulum, the dowser became heavier and heavier. I could actually see them being stripped of their evil forms and evaporating into the light.

As the crystal began to slow down my hand was aching with the strain. A voice came to me with a warning. 'Don't let the pendulum drop on the table, His energy will escape.' My legs went wobbly from having channeled through such a vast amount of energy. It had knocked the wind from my sails. I went weak and for a couple of seconds, I feared I might faint.

As I placed the pendulum carefully in its velvet case, I made eye contact with Joseph. Not showing him an inch of weakness, I glared at him and walked three feet forward to stand in front of his chair.

'Don't worry,' I said with an intimidating tone. 'You're next Joseph.'

He looked furious as he grappled with Kevin's body to get to me. My guides had locked him to the chair.

I watched him clumsily struggle to release himself from the hold they had on him. 'Do you see the dowser sitting on the table? Well it's quite surprising how powerful it is.' I looked at him. ' Joseph, it's time for you to take a good long look around. You're about to say goodbye to your precious Wheatsheaf. You won't be seeing it again any time soon.'

With anger he broke the hold of the guides. He jumped up knocking me backwards, I tried to stay on my feet, but tripped over my own feet, landing on the floor. He glared into my eyes; I could see the hatred he had towards me.

'You fucking whore,' he shouted, stepping closer towards me.

Quickly jumping up from the floor, I didn't dare move from the spot where I was now standing, once again we were eye to eye. I couldn't afford to turn my back on this monster.

'You are going to die.' The words he spat at me were like daggers of fear stabbing me in the heart. For a split second I was frightened to see what his next move was going to be. He slowly stepped one foot back, still holding his intense glare. All I could do was take deep breaths and wait. Intensity was filling the room; from the corner of my eye I could see fourteen witnesses hoping they wouldn't see my murder. They sat filled with terror.

Abruptly, he turned to his right and left the safe zone. All eyes watched him walk back into the darkness to sit in his corner.

I let out the biggest sigh and looked up at the ceiling. 'Thank you angels for giving me this reprieve.'

Everyone broke into excited chatter. They all discussed what they had seen but couldn't believe.

'Oh my heart was in my mouth,' Sam blurted out as she stood up from the chair. 'I haven't felt this tense since I last gave birth.'

'Something like that,' Phil laughed. They now took a quick break from the horrendous events for a bit of humour. I turned and quickly grabbed the nearest chair to take the weight off my shaky legs.

'Aye, you did good there Suzanne,' came Auntie's voice. I looked up to see everyone's concerned expressions, they tried to give me a smile to sooth my nerves.

'I am quite shaken up but I know it's coming to an end soon'. I rested my head on the arm of the chair and watched Chris and Phil as they broke away from their seats. 'Are you both alright?'

They both nodded a yes. Joseph was sitting head down and quiet. I could quite imagine that he was resting and regenerating his energy levels.

'Can we have ten minutes?' Chris asked.

Quickly checking Kevin was still sitting quietly, I agreed that we needed a quick break and a regroup. We tried to console our minds and emotions as much as we could. It was time to draw him back in the circle. Everyone returned to their seats, hoping the whole ordeal would soon be over with.

Loathing

'Are you two okay to continue?' I looked at Phil and Chris. They simultaneously nodded that they were. I gave the group a minute to make themselves comfortable, I wanted everyone to think of happy thoughts and to ask the higher angels to come and haul Joseph's sorry excuse for a ghost out of the pub once and for all.

Stepping out of the safe zone, I walked through the darkness heading towards him. He was still sitting on the back seat against the wall. Nearing him, I noticed slight changes in his body language for the first time in hours. I could see a glimpse of Kevin peering out of Joseph. His shoulders had slumped slightly and some of his features seemed to show stronger. I had hoped Joseph's energy would tire as he worked at commanding Kevin's body and kept up with his attack on me at the same time. *Oh thank God he is weakening*! This was the development I needed to spur me on. It gave me immense strength to see this long running nightmare through. I was not out of the woods yet, but I could see Joseph's demise was near.

'Come on Joseph, let's finish this!' I shouted at him as I leaned towards him. The table was the only obstacle between us. My hands were gripping the wood around its rim. I glowered at him. 'I may have won the last battle with you,' I paused as I slowly leaned within inches of his face. 'Now I am back to win this war!!' As I stepped back, I looked down to see my heated hand prints lie briefly on the surface of the tabletop, then evaporate away. We stood there in a silent stand-off, each trying to stare the other down. More than sick of waiting for a response, I made a hasty decision. *Right, it's now or never!* I flipped the table out of my way and reached for him. Yanking him out of his seat, I walked him quickly across the lounge towards the safe zone, before Joseph could manipulate Kevin's body to stop me.

'I have only one intention on my mind tonight Joseph, just one.' I held on to the front panels of Kevin's jacket. 'To drag you to the pits of hell where you belong.' I looked straight into his eyes. 'Believe me, I will escort you there myself if need be!'

He glared at me, I could feel his anger building up like a pressure cooker. 'Well, if that's where you belong... then watch out Lucifer here we come. Hell will never be the same! In all my days, I have never felt so much hatred for someone, the way I do for you!'

Dragging him to his seat in the safe zone, I had to force him to sit down amongst the rest of the group. I started to interrogate him, calling him all the bastards under the sun. My intention was to make him ferociously angry. I wanted to burn his candle at both ends. Weakening his strength and decaying his energy would enable me to cast him down into the dowser like the rest of his motley crew.

I picked up the velvet pouch from the table and pulled out the pendulum. Placing the crystal between my right thumb and index finger, I held the dowser tight between my fingers. I was prepared. I wasn't about to let his energy go this time. He wouldn't have the luxury of fading and running to the cellar. I needed to end this then and there.

Sitting on the chair opposite me, watching my every move, he didn't retaliate towards me. I felt that, in some way, he knew he would have to leave Kevin's body. He was his own worst enemy, his hatred of me had helped to evaporate his strength. Seeing the power of the pendulum disperse the energy of his puppet pals had frightened him to the core.

I closed my eyes and asked for all the angels from the heavens above to come down and form a circle. Calling for the higher powers to release pure evil out of The Wheatsheaf, I felt the dowser begin to spin around and around. The weight became unbearable immediately, but in the back of my mind I knew I had to hold on.

'I call upon the archangels to remove Joseph from this pub. Drown out his noxious energy. Take back this pub from the clutches of this evil manifestation!'

He started to call me names which would make most blush.

I could feel his panic as I called out for all the help I could draw upon, from God to angels to guides. 'All please come and send him to another dimension.'

'I will never leave you alone,' he spat at me.

I quickly opened my eyes to see him peering out of Kevin's body.

'You rotten bitch... die in hell.' His voice was now a pathetic growl.

With Joseph's outburst of hatred for me, I could feel his energy weakening further. His voice was changing, I could hear Kevin's accent becoming more prominent in the undertones of his speech. This discovery felt like a breath of fresh air to me. *Thank you angels and guides.*

Suddenly, I felt as though I was being pulled into the fierce spinning dowser. My body was freezing as I moved closer to Joseph. Once again, the bright orb of light returned, it's power began to force Joseph's energy from within Kevin. There was a majestic force with me at that moment. It was the first time that I had felt a touch from God. That comforting feeling was in drastic comparison to what happened next.

Visions with crystal clear clarity rushed through my mind. Glimpses of Joseph running the pub all those years ago, flashed by. As more prominent flashes of light engulfed my mind, a horrifying vision came, spinning me back in time. I could see Joseph escorting men down a long corridor with three rooms at the far end. He led them into the rooms, taking their money. The next series of images knocked me sick. The visions were just sporadic flashes this time, like a series of snapshots. I could see women with terrifying distorted faces trapped within a scream. A young girl beaten and bleeding, pleading for the pain to end.

The pictures now came at speed, like a reel of film which showcased the worst of human nature. Emaciated men, heads down, women destroyed by the perverted needs of the twisted. Each frame of this movie depicted hopelessness and terror, brought by Joseph's greed. I saw the early dispatch of those he had no further need for. His past was flashing before my eyes and I now knew the truth. I had known he'd run a brutal and dirty brothel, but I had underestimated his depravity. His need for financial gain was much stronger than his care for humanity. He destroyed anything and anyone who stood in his way.

The last of the visions were too much to bear. Skeletal children, sobbing with the pain of hunger, reached for me. Finally, I saw bodies wrapped in burlap sacks and the crunch of a spade as it dug into the earth, digging holes to swallow the dead.

As the tears streamed down my face, I realized that seeing the full truth was the breakthrough I needed. With the last vision of the midnight grave digger tossing bodies into holes like bits of rubbish fading, I opened my eyes to see Kevin clearly returned to his body and Joseph's drained ghostly energy. The exposed truths had rendered him defenceless from the light glowing within the crystal attached to the pendulum.

He began to scream pathetically.

I felt triumphant seeing the abject fear fill his cowardly face. His wails of terror were the sound of poetic justice. He was forced into the heart of the crystal, but as I suspected, he wasn't done with me yet. The force of the swinging pendulum painfully weighed me down. I felt myself being sucked into the dowser. Joseph's claws sank deeper into my core. He wanted to draw my soul out and take me with him on his journey to the flaming abyss. I fought with everything I had against the magnetic pull of the pendulum. As tears continued streaming down my face, I recalled the vision of the sobbing, skeletal children, and allowed myself to replace my sadness with loathing of his deeds.

Again, the orb began traveling around the pub, absorbing every particle of negativity in its path. Leaving traces of love and light in its wake, it began to swell. The more it extruded the evil energy the bigger it became; I was filled with panic thinking I would be unable to hold the pendulum's weight and momentum. *'This is the final stage, don't let go until the orb is back in the pendulum,'* whispered my guides. I tried to avert my thoughts from the pain in my arm and hand to concentrate on the light itself. In terror, I realized I couldn't locate the glowing light and felt my heart sink. Joseph now had his evil hands clutched around my heart. Just as I felt my arm and hand, involuntarily, about to let go of the pendulum, I noticed the light come flowing down the stairs and head straight towards me. The pendulum was spinning so wildly, it began to make a howling sound.

I could hear gasps from the group as they heard the pendulum's wailing lament, but I had to prevent myself from being distracted. With every frenetic spin of my crystal, his energy was evaporating into a mist. I felt a surge of fear in my soul, as I realized Joseph was standing right in front of me. With an ungodly scream, his face contorted as he rushed towards me. Each word he spoke next, was long and drawn out.

'I… will… come… back… for… you!!!' These were to be the last words he said to me. My crystal weighed heavy, as my arm began shaking with muscle fatigue and tension. I was worried the pendulum's crystal would snap in half under the weight it was carrying. I was frightened that Joseph still had a connection to my mind. Feeling as though I was walking over a frozen deadpool, my feet about to break through the fragile surface, I could hear the ice fracturing into weak points underneath me. I closed my eyes tightly and could see a worm hole of colorful lights appearing above my head. The tension was now lifting in the safe zone, the air was becoming lighter. I took a deep breath and absorbed the clear air transcending the room. I could hear a horse galloping in the background as my mind raced back to Archangel Michael helping me fight Joseph a few days back. I was seconds away from luring the last of his energy into the dowser. At the front of my mind, I was able to see a large ball of light hovering over me. Taking in a cleansing breath, the light entered my aura. My mind became alive with the most awe inspiring colours. They began to swirl and meld around me, cloaking me with love and peace. The light had come to calm Joseph and take him to his Maker.

I let out a gasp of air as the pendulum began to slow down. I bent my head down and opened my eyes. 'Oh God,' I said as I raised my head up to the ceiling. 'Thank you, I am forever in your debt.' For the first time in months, I could actually breathe. Feeling the pressure lift from my body left me with a sense of relief and peace.

'It's over,' I gushed to the fourteen individuals around me. Tears and relief embraced every one of us.

I looked at Kevin sitting in the chair within the circle. His body language told me he was unaware of why he was there. He looked frightened, like a rabbit caught in headlights. He looked totally drained, as though he had gone through ten rounds in a boxing ring. He opened his hands, placing them on the top of his head.

'What the hell is going on?' he looked at me.

I was intrigued to hear Kevin's version of events while they were still fresh in his mind. We moved to a table away from the rest of the group. The last thing he needed was a million and one versions of the story from everyone at once. I felt it was better coming from myself. It would also give me a chance to see if he had any visions or flashbacks from Joseph's energy which might tie in to my visions over my time in The Wheatsheaf.

'I've pulled you aside to explain what has had happened to you tonight'. I slowly sat in the chair opposite him. For the first time since meeting Kevin, I felt relaxed in his company. I began to break it down for him, and told the story of what had happened to me and the group over the past weeks. As I was describing certain experiences in the pub, I felt like a light had switched itself on inside my mind. *My God Suzanne, It's shocking to remember all of what we had actually been through.* I let out a sigh and carried on talking to Kevin. When I got around to explaining that night's events, he stopped me and began to share the few memories he had from the evening. I could see the penny was dropping in his train of thought.

He looked up at me. 'Are you telling me... a ghost possessed my body?'

I had no other explanation and decided to tell Kevin the truth. He shook his head in disbelief. I felt I was still in shock myself, I felt lightheaded and shaky. We had all lived through an ordeal that night. Little speckles of colour started coming back to his cheeks. Kevin was looking more like himself. I asked if he remembered anything happening in the lounge.

'No,' he said, as he shook his head. 'All I remember is going to the toilets, then as I was walking out I heard loads of shouting coming from the room down the hall.' He was trying to think back to earlier this evening as he stroked his head for comfort. 'I was listening to your voice through the white door on the right. Then I heard a man shouting. At that point I turned the handle and popped my head around the door to see if there was anything I could help with. I remember vaguely talking about some bricks, then nothing. I don't remember anything else.'

I couldn't do any more than to leave him to come to terms with the personal ordeal he had experienced that night.

The Light

I slowly began to relax. I'd forgotten how relaxed felt. It had become a sought after luxury. I glanced at the time, 5.30 a.m. Time had literally flown by that night. I invited Kevin to join the rest of the group. I wanted nothing more than to go home and put this nightmare behind me.

The group were buzzing with excitement after defeating Joseph for the second time. Sam and Phil lit the mood with their brilliant sense of humour. The pub was at peace, everyone noticed the change instantly. I asked Chris and Phil if they were feeling better.

'Yeah loads better. The shakes have gone, so anything after that is a bonus.'

I smiled to see Chris was trying to make a light-hearted joke to ease the torture they both had been through. I looked at Phil. He just gave me a nod and a smile to say he was fine.

Comments were flying. 'I can't get over what I have just witnessed Suzanne.' 'You're one brave lass for what you have done here tonight.'

I let out a genuine smile. 'Thank you everyone it's been a night to remember, I couldn't have done it without all your help.'

They had exhaustion written all over their faces. As the night came to a close, I found myself hugging everyone at the doors.

'Have you got everything Suzanne?' Aunty asked as I picked up my bag. After a quick peruse I noticed I'd left behind a notebook and my files. 'I will be two minutes. I told everyone to hang fire as I went up the stairs. Approaching the top flight, I caught sight of a shadow on the top landing. I gasped. I wasn't expecting to see any more specters. I froze as the shadow began to emerge into a ball of light. It slowly moved through the lofty space of the stairwell, floating in midair. I was frightened and curious at the same time. I was in two minds, to stay or to run back down stairs. As I looked closer, I could see little wings on either side. It hovered past the toilets and headed down the corridor towards the room on the right. I slowly followed the light as it disappeared through the door. I

THE LIGHT

walked up the two steps, then held the door handle in my hands hesitating. I turned the handle. The light was directly in front of me as I opened the door fully. The subtle blue light of an autumn morning trickled through the bay windows. I glanced at the floor to see the dark colored carpet had been replaced by floorboards. The familiar Indian tapestry rug was in the middle of the floor. I glanced around to see I was in a kitchen. The table and chairs sat near the center of the room, my heart raced as I noticed Jessica standing next to them. My eyes filled with tears.

'Oh my love.' As I walked closer to her, I thought back to our first encounter at the top of the stairs back in September. It felt like a lifetime since I had been fortunate enough to be next to her. She moved closer to me and held something out in her tiny fingers. She gingerly placed it in my hands. It was a silver necklace, ever so tiny and delicate.

'I found my locket.' She smiled.

I looked at her in more detail and could see the markings of her blindfold around her eyes. 'Turn around little one, let me help you to take off your blindfold.'

She stepped a foot towards me and slowly turned her body to face the window. I stroked her hair as my hand came within her energy. After untying the knot with trembling hands, the blindfold evaporated away in my fingers.

'Your tears are my tears now little soul, go and find peace.'

She turned to me and for the first time I could see the light blue in her eyes. She smiled then vanished.

As the room went back to its present decor, I found myself sitting on the floor in floods of tears, my heart was breaking in two. 'How would I even begin to imagine moving on from this ordeal.'

We all should be honoured in some little way for deeds done that run above the call of duty. The people around me at The Wheatsheaf who witnessed its horrors will be forever commemorated in my heart for their loyalty and bravery. From the preparation, to the bitter end, their dedication spoke volumes in my eyes.

It was going to be difficult to walk away from something as horrific as this had been. Just as tough, was the worry about losing touch with the people who had stood behind me so faithfully. Only they understood fully how hard it had been surviving this ordeal. The memories themselves would be scrutinized by all of us for years to come. If we never saw each other again, we all had the same shared experiences. I'm sure we all hoped that the horrors we had witnessed would never be repeated. We could never do this again in this lifetime.

I loved them all for standing by me.

To be Continued